Cryptid

Lana Szabo

Chapbook Press

Schuler Books
2660 28th Street SE
Grand Rapids, MI 49512
(616) 942-7330
www.schulerbooks.com

Cryptid

ISBN 13: 9781957169453

eBook ISBN: 9781966196372

Library of Congress Control Number: 2023908758

Printed in the United States by Chapbook Press.

"I will not put a name to what has no name."

– Shirley Jackson

Chapter 1

They spotted a party store up ahead, which gave them a shared sigh of relief; they weren't sure if there were even going to be businesses anywhere so remote. The store, built to look like cabin, was dwarfed by the surrounding Black Lake State Forest, as all things around there were. Its shelves were spaced with nearly a foot between inventory, a sparseness the walls made up for with a surplus of Up North paraphernalia: carved wooden bears, resin fish plaques, and crisscrossed skis covering the wallpaper beyond recognition. They needed to pick up beer, which they could keep chilled by leaving outside. The near freezing temperature had turned out to be a plus once they realized that the refrigerator in the cabin had been unplugged for months, otherwise they would have been drinking warm beer for at least the first night. While the rest of Michigan basked in the warmth of a second summer, the group had entered a cold snap after passing the 49th parallel. The North was a picture of October itself, with red, brown, and yellow leaves rustling against a backdrop of blue cut with blustery, fast clouds. The sunset sharpened the cold, which their bodies were unused to after the downstate warmth. They moved quickly from the van into the store, slamming the doors shut behind them and whooping as they ran inside to the shop worker's polite disinterest.

"Should we get some firewood?" asked Brooke.

"We're going into the middle of nowhere, where no one will hear us scream. It will be nothing but us and trees for miles and miles," said Ann with a directness that sounded severe to anyone that did not know her. "We will be surrounded by free wood."

"But it will all be wet if that storm they were talking about on the radio hit up here, we need dry wood. Maybe we should buy some now and then bring some inside to dry out for tomorrow," suggested Mark.

"Or if it snows," added Benny.

"Snow doesn't effect wood burning," said Moody, and then, "Or does it?"

"It snowed in Saginaw a few days ago, they got two inches," said Brooke over her shoulder as she stared into the beverage cooler, stymied by the obscure brands.

"Okay, let's get a few bundles of firewood on top of the beer. And wine. And let's get one bottle of something fun. *Fireball*," said Kaela with an eyebrow raised.

"And ice, right?" asked Benny.

"How about ice and a case of bottled water," said Tom.

"And headache medicine," said Mark forebodingly.

The cashier turned his head to the side and laid his large, heavy eyes on Mark, his face slack from long periods of disuse. He nodded and lifted a finger towards a rack of single use tablets to the side of the register. Mark grabbed eight, almost clearing the entire stock. "I'll get one for each of us, and one extra to be on the safe side."

"Everyone put all of their stuff together, let's buy it all at once so that we can evenly divide what we owe at the end of the trip," said Ann.

The cashier followed them outside and loaded the firewood in the back of their van. Even though it was only a weekend trip they had packed it solid after adding each person's food, clothes, toiletries, and bedding, plus camping equipment in case they decided to camp in the woods or on the island. The back being so dense with supplies, the clerk had to cram the wood on top of the pile, sending splinters shedding down across their belongings.

They started back on their drive to Kaela and Tom's dad's cabin and were momentarily silent as they continued down the highway, feeling collectively unsettled and excited by how far away from their everyday lives they were. Without the use of their phones and not knowing anyone in the area, they were entirely dependent on the functioning of the van. A tire blowing out, a quick fix in the city, would leave them stranded on the side of the road. The isolation became impossible to ignore as they neared the end of their road trip. They did not pass another car for the remainder of the drive and the cabins they passed were unlit from the inside, their residents either not home or moving unseen within. The peak fall foliage slowly dimmed into shadow and the dark chill stoked their riled silence even more. The crisp nitrogen smell rising from the forest was invigorating and a little unsettling, even with sights unseen, their vision weakened by the headlights.

After a few minutes passed the charged silence lapsed into an awkward one and as one person became restless, the antsiness spread. No one had been to the cabin in several months, maybe a year since Kaela and Tom's dad had moved down South. It was time that someone checked on the property, which consisted of a cabin, a boat, and a small island. Kaela felt like Cat would have enjoyed the idea of the group going on this trip together. This did not seem to matter so much to the rest but, still, they had agreed to come, and all that mattered was that they were there. The van quietly turned off the highway and started down the miles of dirt road.

"Let's listen to *Donnie Darko*. It's perfect for right now," said Benny as he reached for the front console to put on music.

Drawn-out notes began to tremor from the speakers and the others took in the music, slowly realizing that it was the movie's thematic score, not the soundtrack. The whining, elongated sounds squealed from the speakers and it became an unspoken challenge to see who could last the longest without breaking. It was a ridiculous music choice that was, strangely, perfect. They smirked to themselves and nobody said anything for the entirety of the first song. Kaela managed not to crack a smile as she asked, "Did I ever tell you guys how Goat Island got its name?"

"I assumed it's because it's where your family sacrifices goats?" said Moody.

"Better," she said, setting off to tell a well-worn story from her family lore. "You see, there were two things that they always say my Uncle Dwayne loved most: drinking and dynamite. Our grandparents would always invite family up here in the summer and Dwayne got his hands on some TNT, don't ask me how–"

"How?" asked Brooke.

"It was the 60's and he worked in a junkyard. Maybe they had that kind of thing around to explode garbage."

"Why would junkyards blow up trash?" asked Ann.

"Who fucking knows, but he loved huge explosions and he took a rowboat out to the island without telling anyone what he was up to, stuck a bunch of sticks of dynamite around a hill and then blew it up to watch the dirt fly everywhere. But the sound was crazy loud, people heard it back at the cabin which is like a mile away, and then after a few minutes there was this stampede of goats running him down. It turned out that a farmer's goats had gotten loose and walked across the lake, because the ice was still mostly solid. But then the last of the ice melted and they were trapped on the island. Nobody knew they were there and Dwayne had to row back to the cabin and explain to everyone what he had done and about the pack of wild goats. A 'trip' of goats."

"Are the goats still there?" asked Benny.

"No, they figured out who the farmer was and rescued them somehow."

"It's hard to have all of the details when you're making something up," said Benny.

"No, this really happened! Everyone that was around can vouch for this story, they tell it all the time. Tell them, Tom."

"It's true," said Tom, "Uncle Dwayne loved drinking and dynamite, and there was a stampede of goats on the island back in the 60's."

Satisfied, Kaela shifted into navigation mode. "Turn left at the next crossroad and then we'll have to keep our eyes out for the driveway. It might be hard to spot right away. Hopefully the front gate isn't overgrown with weeds."

Chapter 2

The gravel crunched under their tires and the chill in the air focused their senses. None of them lived up north but a few had grown up in woodsy neighborhoods and were familiar with signs of nocturnal animals. The bright discs reflecting at them, movements from ground to eye level, antlers moving between the shadows of branches. The silence threatened to take hold again and, in a rare flash of showmanship, Kaela dove into a second story.

"I should probably tell you guys about the Dogman, we *are* in his territory up here." No one objected and she continued. "Dogman is like a mix of a human and a wolf, and they've only been seen in the upper Lower Peninsula, like in this exact area. They're probably up in the UP, too, but there's less people up there to see them and tell people about it. I'm not messing with you, Dogmen have been spotted in these very woods. Nobody knows exactly what they are, well, some people think they're shapeshifters that got stuck mid-shift, but we know what they look like. They're huge, like seven feet tall, with a human body but the face of a Huskey or German Shephard, a breed with a long snout, nothing flat like a Pug face. Wolfy but not a wolf. They walk like people, on two feet, but the feet are like a dog's hind paws, so they leave pawprints, not footprints. That's probably what makes them so hard to track, and people have been trying to track them for a long time. Their eyes are blue or yellow and look like they glow. And they don't talk, either because they can't, or won't, but their screams sound just like a human's."

Benny rolled his eyes.

"They come out once every ten years on the seventh year, like 1907, 1917, 1927. One year, it had to be either 1967 or 1977, a group of hippies came up here to go camping. They had one of those vans that was all blinged out with a mural on the side, bean bags and a lava lamp in the back, and they were going to camp by sleeping in the van at night. They were partying, drinking some beers, smoking some pot, singing hippy songs while someone played the guitar, and then one girl stepped outside to get some fresh air. She was looking around the woods and saw something glinting between some trees. She kept looking at it, trying to figure out what it was because it wasn't moving at all but was super bright. Once her eyes adjusted she realized it was a pair of eyes staring back at her but before she could react the light flicked away, so she figured it was just a raccoon or a deer, the type of animal that would be derpy enough to stand there staring at people for no reason.

"She went back in the van and didn't mention it, figuring it was nothing. Later they settled into their sleeping bags and then, after they fell asleep, there was this sound that kept almost waking them up. You know what I mean, when you're sleeping but you hear a train in the distance or a door creaking, and it wakes you up just a little? But then you fall back asleep and use dream logic to explain it, or it even becomes part of the dream? This was like that but with a scratching sound, like something slowly scraping against the side of the van.

"It was windy outside so even when it woke them up a little they assumed it was something like a branch scratching against the window making the sound. Then one of them couldn't get back to sleep and got up to look out the window and see if he could figure out what was making the sound. And he saw this mangy dog face with bright blue eyes looking right at him through the window. The guy was still half asleep and thought it was some kind of dog stretching up against the window but as he looked it over he saw that it had the body of a man, a naked man. Then it showed him its teeth, like he was trying to smile ear to ear, and the guy screamed. This completely woke up the rest of the hippies and everyone saw the Dogman in the window right before he took off. They lost their shit and drove away. But when they got home nobody believed them. Well, people up here believed them, but nobody else did."

"Does Dogman eat people?" asked Benny, a generous question considering he did not believe a word of it.

"No, in the legends the Dogmen are more about scaring people than eating them," said Kaela authoritatively, pleased by the question.

"I like his style," said Mark.

"Hey, it's 2017. Maybe we'll see Dogman," said Brooke excitedly, and then the group quieted once more as they rolled to a stop in front of a row of bushes.

Kaela and Tom hopped out of the van, pulling the bush branches aside to reveal the gate to the driveway. It was overgrown with ivy and weeds but surprisingly easy to move to the side, the grasses giving way without protest. The driveway itself was more of a suggestion, knee high with weeds and grass. They slowly pressed the van through the path, easing over the bumps and hidden holes. Each of them grit their teeth and squinted into the trail lit before them, paranoid of Mark driving into a tree that had unexpectantly taken root in the way. Everyone was too focused to stop the movie score, which now consisted of a long reverberation of a theremin's high note.

"Dogman would be easily neutralized by a well-aimed steak," whispered Moody as they reached the halfway point of the driveway.

"You know what would be the scariest thing we could pull up on?" asked Brooke, startling the rest by speaking at a normal volume.

"What?" asked Kaela as she struggled to see ahead, which was difficult even with headlights. There was no one around to help if they got stuck, and it wouldn't be a matter of just jarring the van loose if it got entangled; it would be a rat's nest of gnarls in every direction. They moved forward cautiously as branches snapped along the windows and sides of the van. Piles of leaves had accumulated, causing them to rise and fall as wheels crushed the mounds underfoot. Each word set a shiver up their spines as Brooke said, "A middle aged man."

"Shit," said Benny, "that really would be the worst thing, wouldn't it?"

"What about a little girl ghost?" said Mark.

"Or a super old grandma?" said Moody.

"Or a baby--" said Benny.

"No dead baby jokes," said Ann, nipping it in the bud.

It was a moonless night and growing cloudier by the minute, so it was hard to make out the frame of the cabin during their approach. It was one story, but with high ceilings on the side wings. It looked small at first glance but extended further back than expected; extensions had been added over the years. The front façade was part of the original cinderblock construction and held a heavy wooden door, which was standing ajar, giving a peek into the further darkness.

"Hold on," said Tom. "That door shouldn't be open. Remember how many locks are on that front door?"

"A family of raccoons probably picked the lock to eat Dad's trash. Or maybe it was left open by accident. *Chillax,*" said Kaela as she eased out from the passenger seat. Tom and Mark got out first, opening and shutting their doors in near unison.

Tom called out "That deadbolt's been on there since the fifties, no animal broke in. We need to make sure it's safe inside, all together."

"Safety in numbers," agreed Mark.

"S.I.N.," said Kaela.

The atmosphere shifted now that they were parked and the music was turned off. As they stepped out of the van their eyes began to adjust and they took in their surroundings. To their left was a bonfire pit surrounded by tree stumps fashioned into stools, a wooden shed leaning its weight onto the tree next to it, a green-roofed aluminum shed, and a sturdy birch tree holding sentry between them with a hatchet wedged into its trunk. The air smelled of pine and there was a bite to each breath they took. The sky was emptied of light and the woods were a gradient of darkness and even darker shadows. There was a group sensation of tempered danger, as though something could go wrong but surely nothing too extreme.

"Okay, let's sweep the cabin all together, Tom is right," said Ann as she balanced a tree branch over her shoulder like a baseball bat. The others took her meaning and armed themselves with flashlights and keys between their knuckles as they formed a single file line towards the front door. The van's headlights timed out, clicking off as Tom nudged the door further open.

"If there is anyone in there, even if it's an old hippy and he's like 'hey guys, I just thought I'd stay here while no one was around, I'll be on my way', I'm going to beat him to death with this," said Brooke, holding up a two by four she had found near the wood pile.

Nobody said anything in response as they stepped inside, each of the others shifting around Tom to make sure he remained in the front out of an archaic sense of whose duty it was to die in defense of the cabin. Leaves cracked under their feet and their flashlights illuminated piles of natural debris that had found its way indoors; nuts and acorns swept inside by the wind, odd bits left over from animals scavenging, spider-webs, and dirt. They moved through quietly at first, exploring the rest of the rooms together in a tight knot. Benny walked into a lamp and tried to turn it on, clicking it around futilely.

"We have to find the circuit breaker," said Kaela, making Brooke jump.

They pressed into the far side of the house which housed the two bedrooms. The cement block walls shifted to white plaster which then gave way to wood paneling as they angled their flashlights into each corner, the beams creating a maelstrom of shadows rather than one cohesive light. Bedroom mattresses smelling of mildew were stacked in one corner of the master bedroom, with rolls of yellowed wallpaper leaning in against the other. The clutter gave both corners the initial look of something crouching in their peripheral vision.

Tom pulled out a flashlight and went out the backdoor to start up the generator, taking a cannister of gas with him. After a few minutes he called out for them to try the lights, which flickered on hesitantly. "The generator should be fine through the weekend as long as we don't run too much stuff all at once."

They only turned on a couple of lamps, careful not to overwhelm the system. The light in the den beamed up to showcase a deer head mounted on the wall and detritus shone throughout the cabin; old newspapers flattened into rug fibers and the couch covered in animal droppings, but it was an otherwise a cozy cabin. It had undeniable potential for good times to be had.

"It doesn't look like anyone's been in here. I mean, there's some trash around, but that could easily be from my dad," said Kaela.

They began to bustle about, half of them clearing the mounds of weathered trash and sweeping the floors while the other half went out to collect their bags. Ann put on music before anyone else could make the selection, choosing the Beastie Boys *Licensed to Ill* out of the dusty cd collection. She shook off cobweb strands and blew off the lid before placing the disc inside the tiny boombox.

"Hey, it's starting to rain. We'll pull the rest of the stuff inside but I don't think we'll be able to have a bonfire tonight." said Mark from the doorway as he chucked a finished cigarette to the side.

Kaela walked up from the rear of the house as she said, "Another thing is, it seems like something has been either living inside or around these mattresses. I'm really sorry guys, but whatever has been living in here has been peeing on this stuff for a while. It looks like critters have been coming in from the back door, too, because it's actually just held shut by a bungee cord, he never got around to installing a lock after adding this addition. The cord is loose and the door was open a few inches."

"I bet Bigfoot has been squatting here," said Mark.

"Or Dogman," said Moody.

"Do not bring him up again. It might be a 'Madman Marz' situation where if we keep saying his name he'll show up," said Kaela, referencing *Madman*, the movie she and Mark had watched the night previous to get pumped for the trip, and Mark snorted in appreciation.

"If Dogman sticks his face in the window all we have to do is ignore him," said Brooke. "He's pretty much a harmless Peeping Tom."

Ann redirected them to the business at hand. "I'm thinking it might be best to actually sleep on our airbeds instead of risking it any of these mattresses. They might even be able to fit on the bed stands instead of the mattresses."

"Except, we don't know if any animals are still inside the cabin, inside those mattresses, for example. I don't want to wake up with a weasel on my face," countered Mark.

"Let's set up the tents inside," said Kaela. "Then sleep on the airbeds inside the tents."

"Yeah. You know, it's not a big deal to set things up in here. It isn't like we're going to be hanging out inside much anyway. I feel like if anyone sits on the couch for too long a bunch of bats are going to come flying out," said Benny.

They were able to fit three tents inside the den after moving the furniture against the walls. A fourth tent was set up in the larger bedroom, with there being enough room once they had moved the soiled mattresses and bed frames aside to the smaller room. Tom luckily found a spare tent stuffed into a back closet (he had refused to buy one, assuming that he would find something usable once they got to the cabin). He set up his camp on the opposite side of the bedroom, underneath the small, curtainless window. Shutting the door to the room gave the sense of being shut off from the world, the wood of the door sealing perfectly with the wood grain walls, and even Tom left the door open, as private as he was.

"This will actually be kind of fun. And we could still all hang out and watch a movie, it isn't that late yet," said Brooke.

"As long as the spiders don't mind the noise," said Moody.

"You mean as long as the ghosts don't mind the noise," said Kaela.

Rain began pelting down on the rooftop and the trees, the van looking completely desolate, a hunched sentinel standing watch in front of the soaking wet woods.

"It didn't even call for rain, I hope this doesn't go on all weekend. My phone has no signal. Can anyone get a signal to check on the weather?" asked Kaela. A quick check revealed that nobody had a signal, their cut off from society complete.

"This is good, it means no one can get involved in work bullshit or social media," said Brooke cheerily.

"Except some of us kind of need to check on work stuff," said Ann.

"Or have to check on our websites," said Mark.

"I'm sorry guys, but we really can't control there not being internet up here," said Kaela.

"Yeah, but you told us it probably wouldn't be a problem," said Benny pointedly, his cheeks flushing red.

"There's a library about ten miles from here, we could go there tomorrow for like an hour to check on things. Really guys, it's only two days without phones."

"Lot of whining," mumbled Tom, staring out at the rain through a side window with faded plaid curtains.

"Okay, it's not that big of a deal, right? Let's all get in our pajamas, have some drinks, and relax," said Kaela in the manner of a teacher calming an unruly class.

They began to disperse throughout the cabin, unpacking their bags, setting out food, plugging in the minifridge, and Mark went to turn on the tap water to let the rust run out of the pipes. "Do you have running water here? I'm trying to use the sink faucet but nothing is coming out. Also, it looks like someone took a piss and just left it in the toilet, which isn't flushing."

"*Ohh*. Someone needs to go out to turn on the well pump," said Kaela. Lightning struck nearby, a splitting sound like a tree being ripped in half. Rain pelted the windows in waves and the thunder crashed above their heads. "Or we wait until the storm is over."

Chapter 3

They laid a tarp across the couch in the den, cinching it into the cushions to pin it into position. The room also served as a mudroom and was large enough to house their tents with room to spare in front of the tv, which was in a stand along with a still working VCR, the entire technological setup grandfathered in the 1980's. Kaela and Mark went over to figure out the settings and squabbled over which tape to select from her dad's collection, finally settling on *Body Double*. The group nestled in blankets throughout the room, curled towards the lone space heater, the tarp crinkling beneath each movement made on the couch. Covered in sleeping bags and fleece blankets to ward off the draft creeping in from the edges of the doors, they were still grateful for shelter as the rain cascaded down the roof, giving a sense of coziness regardless of how leaf covered and cobwebbed the cabin may be.

"I'm still going to have smores, fire be damned," said Benny as he smooshed chocolate squares into an uncooked marshmallow between two graham crackers.

"*Shh*," hissed Mark, pointing hard at the tv with his can of Coors Light. His eyes were fixed on the screen as the protagonist of *Body Double* fell into an open grave and began screaming, the shot then panning out to reveal a movie set, the screaming man an actor, and the coffin a prop. "That fucks me up every time."

It was one in the morning and while the rain had slowed it had also thickened, the drops landing with heavy splashes. Tom packed a bowl of Gorilla Glue and said, "I'm going outside to smoke this, come outside if you'd like to partake."

The group watched him duck out the front door, his short black hair and pale white skin making his departure resemble a vampire whose invitation had been rescinded.

"I want to smoke but not with him," said Benny aside to Ann.

"Even if someone else were offering, I'm getting tired. We should probably get some rest before our sleep gets out of whack," Ann murmured back.

"No way, I heard that. You're trying to go to sleep. We never all hang out together. My feelings will be hurt if you fall asleep. Please, Benny," Moody begged, too amped to sleep and disturbed at the prospect of lying awake for hours with nothing to do.

"Okay, you're right, we'll stay up. We should get as much out of this as we can," said Ann with the air of someone determined to get their money's worth on a gamble gone sideways.

"I have a different kind of green you could try… I brought some bottles of absinthe, they have actual wormwood in them. I'm not even sure how they made it through homeland security, I thought for sure they'd get seized. I've haven't tried it yet but it's supposed to fuck you up," offered Mark helpfully.

"Mark, I was hoping someone brought surprise ecstasy. Isn't absinthe what drove Edgar Allen Poe insane?" said Ann.

"Nevermore – I'm sure they've worked out the kinks by now," said Benny. "Let's make some memories."

With that Mark began to dig a bottle out from his bags and started pouring it into red Solo cups. As he passed them out there was a bang on the wall and they turned to see Tom looking in at them from the window. "I think we're supposed to wait for Dracula to come back in before we start," said Mark.

"I guess so," said Ann right before Tom began walking away, only the back of his pale neck visible in the darkness. "But he looks like he's going somewhere."

"Probably to take a piss," said Moody. "Or to jerk off to *Body Double*. That sex club scene got him all worked up."

"He's heading in the direction of the well, he must be going to start the water pump. He could wait until the rain lets up but whatever. Let him do him," said Kaela. "Our dad built that well himself. I mean, he probably had some help, but he did most of it. He kind of made it for Tom and I, since we'll inherit this place someday. He asked us what color of rocks we wanted it made with and we chose white."

"So, it looks like the well from *The Ring*?" asked Brooke.

"... *Fuck*. It does look like the well from the ring." Kaela walked over to the window. "He's over there just staring down into it."

"I've never liked wells," said Brooke. "I always feel like there's going to be someone standing at the bottom, looking up at me. Or that a someone is going to come crawling up out of it and their hand is about to grab me."

"Where does a mansplainer get his water?" Moody asked, paused a beat, and then answered himself, "A well, actually." Brooke gave him an irritated look as she pulled her curly red hair back in a bun.

"Well, call that weirdo inside, we should wait to drink the absinthe until everyone is here. Group bonding and all," said Ann.

"Tom, stop fucking around and come inside," Benny shouted out the front door. Tom walked slowly back and accidentally slammed the door shut behind him, the wind causing a shift in air pressure. The jolt sent something scampering in the ceiling. "Must have woke up a poltergeist."

Mark handed Tom a cup, which he downed without hesitation and followed up with a face like he'd been given straight Popov. "Don't mind him, let's the rest of us toast," said Kaela, looking disapprovingly at Tom. "To Cat, who I'm sure would have loved hearing that we all came up north together."

The absinthe tasted like fire water; gas with a searing afterburn. It left them all teary eyed and hacking, with Kaela, Mark, and Ann futilely trying to scrape the taste off their tongues while Brooke, Moody, and Benny scream-laughed.

There was another thump from the rafters and they took turns guessing what was behind the noise ("A squirrel." "A raccoon?" "A giant spider."). Kaela turned to Tom, "What actually could be making that sound?"

He looked at them, his eyes shiny and his glasses still fogged from being outside, making his already deadpan expression inscrutable. "A mini goat." He paused for a second and then continued, "It looks like the van sunk into some mud. We parked in what must have been a small sinkhole and the rain is making it worse. We'll have to figure something out once the rain stops."

The group digested this news slowly.

"I think at this point we have to admit this trip is cursed," said Ann.

"No, this is good. It's like rain on a wedding day. Good luck, not bad," said Brooke, working to preemptively squash any overly negative reactions.

"Cat would have thought it was funny for sure," said Kaela uncertainly and Benny rolled his eyes. They grumbled collectively about the van but came to a consensus that it was a matter to be resolved in the morning anyway, with the entire outdoors currently a splash zone.

"Hey, do you guys want to hear a scary story? I looked up some CreepyPastas the other day and I think I can remember a few well enough to retell," said Moody.

"We just drank absinthe and there's no way in hell I'm setting foot outside. There's no better time for a scary story, even if you heard it from one of your incel friends," answered Brooke.

"But coming from an incel would make it that much scarier," said Benny.

"You go first, then I have dibs on telling the next story," said Brooke. "We should all tell a scary story, it's the perfect time of year for this kind of thing."

"Okay, this is a long one so hold on to your butts. There was this guy whose uncle had a bunch of land with a couple of trailers set up on it, as like a hunting getaway. One weekend he invited a bunch of his friends to party out there, trying to throw a rager. But, this was all happening before cell phones and it was in a pretty remote location so everyone that wanted to come had to meet at his house and then drive in a caravan to get there. It was around twenty to thirty people and he didn't know everyone that was there but he was okay with friends of friends being invited. The thing is that they couldn't park right next to the trailers because they were set about half a mile into the woods from the road. People had to park next to the road and then walk to the trailers, because, like I said, this was his uncle's hunting getaway – it was isolated on purpose.

"As soon as they got there, the guy, I'm calling him Rick, remembered that uncle telling him there was a huge animal in the woods and warned everyone there might be something like a bobcat or bear around but people laughed it off. Like 'Ha ha, okay Rick.' Then someone pointed out that there was a weird smell in the air, like an electric burn, and they figured it was coming from one of the trailers, like something metallic burning up from exposure. They started partying and after a while some people said they wanted to smoke down while they watched the sunset from down by the river. Some people didn't go and stuck around the bonfire and shot-gunned beers and what-have-you. A little time went on and they smelled that electric smell again, the term the creepypasta used was 'ozone.'

"At first Rick thought it was still something coming from the trailers but couldn't trace where it was coming from. He figured this time it must have been something weird burning up in the fire. Then the people that went to the river came running up the path and ran straight into one of the trailers. They looked really freaked out and slammed the door shut behind them, like they forgot the other people were there and were shouting for them to get inside a trailer through the window to the other people trying to figure out what was going on. When they calmed down they explained that while they were down by the river they saw a carcass on the other side that looked like a coyote torn to shreds. Then, as they were trying to get a good look at it to figure out what it was, they heard a sound coming from the woods. One of them shined a flashlight towards the noise and they could see a silhouette of someone standing between some bushes next to the water.

"They yelled at whoever it was and called him an asshole, thinking it was someone from the party trying to scare them. But they could see that the guy was facing the opposite direction, with his back turned to them. He didn't react to what they said and they were creeped out to the point they started walking away, thinking that whoever it was could find their way back to the camp easily enough, but they kept turning back to see where he was. They didn't see the guy again until they were almost out of sight of the river, then when they turned to look back and he was standing to the side of the path, still facing backwards, and then instinct kicked in and they all took off running. But as they ran they began to hear a gibberish sound coming from the woods to their side and someone stopped to shine their flashlight over and said she saw someone 'jerking himself through the woods.' I remembered that line verbatim, ha. Right as they could see the campfire they heard something crash in the woods behind them, and whatever it was had to know they were headed to the trailers.

"As they explained what happened the electric smell began to get stronger and stronger, but they still thought it was some kind of mechanical malfunction and kept on ignoring it. It didn't seem like a huge deal, and plus, once the group was all back together, there were so many of them that nobody could feel too scared, because a group that big could take on one creeper. And they thought it was probably a local redneck messing with them for cheap thrills. Nobody was scared to the point of leaving and most people suspected that it could have also just be someone from the party taking a prank too far. They were about to go back outside when one guy said that he had heard from a local kid whose family had lived in the area for generations about legends of the Goatman. Nobody wanted to hear it, they just wanted to get back to partying, but he kept telling them about it, how it could look like a person but could take on other appearances, and could even impersonate people.

"He went on for so long that people got more freaked out and began peeking out the windows, trying to see if anyone was outside or watching from the woods. But, since everyone there was packed into one trailer, and there was that burning smell getting worse and worse, they couldn't stay inside for the entire night. After a while went by and they didn't see anyone around they went outside and got back to the bonfire. The smell wasn't as bad outside and people decided that it had to be friends that arrived late, screwing around to scare them. And this was dangerous in its own way because it made them paranoid the rest of the night, expecting people to come flying out screeching from the woods when they least expected it. Nothing else happened that night but some people couldn't sleep from being so nervy.

"The next day a few more people showed up and they hung around all day, playing games, listening to music, having themselves a good time. They were staying up all night and around 1 am they were telling scary stories around the campfire and the smell came back big time. It was so strong that one girl started gagging until she threw up. The air felt cold and clammy and they all headed into the trailers after dousing the fire. But, there wasn't much room for that many people to actually sleep inside, even spread across the two trailers. There were all of the beds and bunk beds set up but there still wasn't a ton of space, so people couldn't really get situated. Half the people just kept partying and the other laid in the beds, but no one could get actual sleep.

"The one guy that kept talking about the Goatman started up again, but by this time he was sloppy drunk and it was getting people upset, plus that horrible smell was coming in. Since no one was actually asleep Rick decided to cook up a couple of packages of hot dogs. He had two packs of six and he boiled them over the stove and told everyone to grab one once they were ready. He did a quick head count and saw there were twelve people in the trailer and announced that it was one hot dog apiece. Everyone slowly got their food, it was a whole mess, everyone reaching around each other for shit. Then there was one guy left without a hot dog. He started popping off about how shitty it was that someone else ate two when everyone else only got one and now he didn't even get a hot dog. Everyone denied it and then one of the girls started screaming,

'It's in here, GET OUT!' She shoved past everyone to get outside and everyone else ran out after her.

"Once they were outside she asked if there was still anyone inside the trailer. Rick went back in and looked around but didn't see anyone, and when he came back out she did a headcount. There were still twelve people total and then some of the people from the other trailer came outside to see what was up. So, it began to get confusing keeping track of who was where. But looking around, it seemed like one of the people that they had seen earlier was missing. Rick said he had seen one guy standing with his back to him while he was eating his hot dog and had assumed it was one of his buddies but looking over his friends, he realized that the other guy's hair was longer than any of theirs. Talking it over they all realized that there had been a guy in the trailer that none of them knew but everyone thought was someone else's friend.

"Nobody remembered talking to him, they just saw him eating and staring off into space. They were looking all over, paranoid about where the guy had gone, explaining to the people in the other trailer what happened, and then it broke out into an argument over whether they should stay or go. Then Sara, which is what I'm naming the girl that first ran out of the trailer, told them that the guy next to her had turned to her, grabbed her knee, looked into her eyes and started speaking gibberish, with completely garbled words. That's when she ran from the trailer. But after talking about it they all decided that they were too drunk and it was too late to go walking through the woods to their cars, so everyone verified that they knew each other and went back into the trailers. At this point they were exhausted so most of them fell asleep while a few people still couldn't.

"As soon as the sun rose some people started packing up and walking to their cars straight off but a handful of people want to sleep in. The people that wanted to get going were like 'no way, we're getting out of here and its best that we move all together in one big group.' Since people mostly felt safe with the daylight, they wound up agreeing to split up and leave at different times instead of everyone moving at once. The girl that the long-haired guy touched was one of the people that were really eager to get out of there. Rick had to stick around until the second group was ready to go since he had to lock up his uncle's trailers, especially if there was a psychopath screwing around. After the first group left, the rest went back to sleep for a few hours and when they got up they still didn't feel a need to rush out of there. They had plenty of time left in the day to get packed up. They all wanted to go down to the river again before leaving.

"But then time got away from them and by the time they started packing up it was late afternoon. Before they started walking back they still had to clean up the trailers or else his uncle wouldn't let him stay out there again. They were all pitching in and cleaning up when one girl pointed outside and said that Sarah must have forgot something because she was standing outside. Rick looked out the window and saw Sarah standing by the fire pit with her back turned to them. Right then the metallic smell came back and he was like 'I think the electric smell is from whoever that person is,' and everyone kind of laughed it off, like he was trying to scare them. He got annoyed and was like 'If you're so sure it's Sarah then go out there and check,' and then one of the girls actually did.

"She walked towards the firepit and said hi and at first Sarah didn't do anything, then all of a sudden she bent over forward and began convulsing but without making any sounds. While they watched they realized that the entire woods were totally silent. Rick yelled to the girl to get away from Sarah and come back to the camper and she started backing up slowly. They were all in one trailer since they'd been cleaning together and they locked the doors, the windows, and closed all the blinds. They were all completely quiet, trying to listen for any movement and to keep tabs on Sarah through the edges of the curtains. She had stopped heaving and went back to standing there with her back turned to them. This went on for several minutes and they also tried to keep watch for anyone that was with her, like maybe there were other people in the woods and she was some kind of decoy, but they couldn't spot anybody.

"One guy turned to say something and right then there was a loud bang on the driver's side door. Everyone froze and someone looked through a side panel and said it was okay, it was their friend John, and Sarah was still near the firepit. John was panicked and jumped inside as soon as they opened the door. He was terrified, asking who the person by the firepit was and why did she look like Sarah. He said that he had dropped Sarah off at home and then drove back to the campsite to hang out another night because his other plans fell through. He said the girl that looked like Sarah had watched him walk up with her mouth hanging open, just staring as he got closer. He kept his distance from her and when his back was turned she began to move slowly towards him, following him with her eyes. When he got to the trailer door and looked behind him she had moved closer without him seeing her take a step.

"Everyone was freaked because it clearly wasn't Sarah outside, it didn't make any sense for her to be there. Then one of the girls got pissed because she thought it was all a prank that Rick and Sarah had come up with. Everyone started arguing, some people saying it was a prank taken too far, or it was locals messing with them on like the level of the murderers from *The Strangers*. And then that one guy started up again, saying maybe it was actually the Goatman. Then one of the guys started saying he was going to run for it to his car, that he refused to spend another night out there, and he was going to run through the entire woods. The others convinced him not to do it because the sun was nearly setting and then that smell of metal on fire came back to the point that people started dry heaving. They looked out the window to try and find the source but there was nobody there, not even whoever it was that looked like Sarah. Nobody wanted to go outside and the reality set in that they would have to spend another night out there.

"People were way more subdued than on the first night, keeping inside and playing cards, trying not to ralph from the smell. Shortly before midnight there was a scratch at the door and this disjointed voice said 'let me in, stop fucking around, let me in.' But it was really unnatural, like the person kept stopping between each syllable. Not stuttering, more like short pauses within the words, searching for the correct sounds to make. Then one of the girls started to make a ton of noise, banging on the table, stomping her feet on the floor, yelling, trying to scare it away like it was a bear. Whatever it was just kept scraping at the door and asking to be let in, and then after a few minutes it finally stopped. Everyone was silent, listening as quietly as they could for what was going on outside without actually opening any windows or doors. They could hear large cracking sounds coming from the woods every so often, like branches being split. Then finally this guy was like 'Man, fuck this!' and started digging around the storage compartment next to the side door until he found something that could work as a weapon, and then he saw a flare gun.

"He went out the door and held the gun out, yelling for whoever it was to come out and show themself, and he didn't see anything but he did hear gibberish echoing from the river, and then there was a screech, like an animal was getting killed. The guy shot off the flare gun in panic and dropped it while he slammed the door shut. There was no way anyone wanted to run through the woods at that point. It was one of those situations when people had been scared for so long that it started to feel normal. Plus, at this point it seemed like it had to be locals fucking with them. At the same time, if it was people that wanted something, they would have robbed them by then, so they weren't sure what the people were even after.

"People were so tired that most fell asleep within the hour, despite being fucking terrified. Rick laid down to try and get some rest but couldn't sleep, he was hyper aware of every noise around him, and then someone came out from the bathroom. He hadn't seen anyone go inside the bathroom and was kind of confused, but figured someone was in there taking a dump for so long that he lost track of them. Whoever it was went and laid down next to someone on a lower bunk but then here and there they would stand up. The beds were really uncomfortable so he was like 'don't freak out, the Goatman isn't a real thing, this guy just needs to stretch.' But it kept happening throughout the night, this guy getting up, kind of jittering around, sometimes doubling over like he was laughing really hard but without making a sound; then after a couple hours he went back to the bathroom and didn't come back out.

"In the morning nobody wanted to screw around again, they got up as soon as the sun came up, packed up, skipped breakfast, and started walking through the woods back to their cars. When everyone started off

Rick said for them to go ahead, that he'd be right behind them, and went to lock everything up and check around for anything damaged or stolen. Everything was fine but then he gave the bathroom a look over and saw that the window was open. It was a window missing its screen, so at a glance it looked like a glass window that was closed. He had no idea how long it had been open but realized that whoever had been fucking with them must have been coming in and out through the window. He got out of the trailer and caught up to the rest of the group and they got out of the woods fine… I guess that's a pretty weak ending."

"No, it's good. Because nobody can tell if it was people or something else. And it could still be there, laying the groundwork for a part two. Well done," said Ann.

"I think his uncle was the Goatman the whole time," said Kaela.

"I think it was a chupacabra," said Mark.

They sat back to ponder the possibilities, and something in the wall seemed to consider it as well, as what sounded like a mouse began to scuttle around and around in a circle. "But it was a creepypasta, right? This never actually happened?" said Kaela.

Moody looked at her blankly. "It could have happened. It could be the one true creepypasta."

"Okay, you did all right. Maybe you went on for a bit long, but we'll give you a pass. Ready yourselves for an actually scary story with the bonus of it also being true, plus I'll keep this short and sweet," said Brooke, clearly excited to share a story rehearsed to perfection. "This was one I heard from a girl that I went to summer camp with when I was a kid. My parents used to send me to this weird camp for a few weeks each summer because they would get sick of me being around all of the time. But I got to know the other kids that were sent there each year and we would bunk in the same cabin together and this girl, Maddy, told us this story.

"She said that she lived with her mom in this small cottage growing up and that her mom was really artsy. Like she taught ceramics at a community college and would have students and other artists over sometimes. Sometimes they would have art parties–"

"I once went to an art party. One guy got so stoned that he tripped over a can of black paint and it spilled everywhere. Everybody's art got covered in paint. I lost my favorite sweater that night," interrupted Moody.

Brooke stared, momentarily thrown, then restarted. "Anyway, there was always a lot of arts and crafts and ceramics going on in their house. One of their favorite things to do was to make masks of their own faces – have you guys ever done that? It's where you cover your face with

Vaseline and then put a layer of clay over that and wait for it to dry, sometimes people even put straws in their nostrils so they can breathe while it sets. When it's completely dry you pull it off the person's face, let it air dry, paint it, and hang it on the wall. One whole wall of their living room was covered with masks of their friends' faces, which is kind of terrifying and awesome all at once, you know? Maybe if it weren't in the den where everyone hung out it wouldn't seem so creepy… But no, because putting them off to the side would be even worse. At least with them hanging in the den people could keep an eye on them. Like if you had a collection of pretty dolls. It's better to line them up so that you can track any movements.

"Maddy said the den was situated so that there was a doorway behind the couch leading to where their rooms were and there was another door to the side of the couch to the kitchen, then inside the kitchen were two doors, one leading to the garage and the other to the backyard. Her mom was really on top of keeping the doors locked since it was just the two of them there. Like, her mom had a lot of friends coming in and out but she still kept things secure.

"One night her mom and one of her friends were hanging out and Maddy was watching tv until it was time for bed. She got up to brush her teeth and noticed her mom going to check the doors to make sure everything was locked, which they usually were anyways. Since it was such a tiny place her mom shut the door to the bedroom hallway and the kitchen door so their conversation didn't keep Maddy up. While she was brushing her teeth, she heard a knock on the kitchen door. She figured it was another of her mom's friends and thought nothing of it. Then she could hear her mom walk to the back door and say, 'Must be at the front door' and then her mom's friend walked across the house to look out the front door and she said, 'There's no one out here, either.'

"Right then her mom started screaming and Maddy rushed out of the bathroom to see what was wrong. Her friend came back into the room like 'What the flip?' and her mom pointed to the wall of masks. Now, some of these were hanging from nails way high up on the wall, it wasn't like you could easily reach all the masks, but something had happened to them. They were all messed up, like covered in ash and black streaks, and one in the corner had a black smudge circled in the forehead of the mask. Maddy's mom was so upset that she accused her friend of having done it somehow while she checked the doors but her friend denied it, saying she had only got up to check the front door while Maddy's mom checked the back. And there wasn't enough time for her to do all of that, we're talking less than a minute from when they heard the knock at the door.

"They thought that someone else must have snuck inside the house and walked around to see if a window was open in the bedrooms or the bathroom but nothing was open or unlocked. They even checked the garage in case someone was hiding in there but didn't find anyone. The only thing that made sense was that someone else had broken in, vandalized the masks, and was still hiding somewhere inside. Her mom said for them to all get outside and they went over to a neighbor's house for the night. The next morning, they went back to check on the house and nothing else was missing or damaged and there were no signs of anyone else having been there. Her mom took a closer look at the masks and could tell that the black stuff wasn't paint or ink, it was more like oil. They started cleaning up the mess and took down all of the masks to clean what could be salvaged. At first it looked like her mom's mask hadn't been ruined until it was taken down. When they turned it around they saw that the inside of the mask, the part facing the wall, was totally singed.

"Then over the course of the next ten years, each friend of her mom that had made a mask that had been damaged got really sick or died. One person was in a fatal car accident, another person drowned while on a canoe trip, and then Maddy's mom died from a rare form of skin cancer. Maddy could never figure out if it was all some sort of prank, or maybe it was a message from something trying to warn them they were in danger, or maybe making the masks the way they did had unleashed some kind of dark magic, or drew it to them. But she never really discussed the masks with people because usually they accused her of making it up. She said she feels really lucky because when she was a kid she was always asking her mom to make a mask of her face but her mom always refused, saying it would be too hard for her to sit still that long. That might have saved her from whatever curse there might have been."

"Is her story over?" Benny asked Ann.

"Yeah, I think so," she answered in a low voice.

"Thank God," he said, mashing his face into his pillow.

A genuine tiredness had settled over the group over the course of the story-telling and they unanimously decided to call it a night and get some sleep, silently tucking into their sleeping bags, regardless of whether or not they slept. The shifting air mattresses gave out rubbery shrieks beneath their bodies accompanied by a cacophony of snores.

One of those lying awake was Kaela, wondering if people were enjoying the trip, if Cat would have enjoyed the trip, if she would have kept people up even longer, if she would have approved of the movie choice, and what would she have said about them pitching tents inside.

Mark went outside to smoke. It was still raining and had dropped into the upper 30's, making his exhales a mixture of smoke and frozen breath. He heard the rain falling from the branches, seeping into the near freezing ground, and relaxed, grateful for a few minutes away from the group. He liked going to the cabin with Kaela but not with all these other people, too. Plus, the absinthe didn't do anything outside of burn his throat; it probably wasn't even real absinthe, another waste of money. He hoped that he'd be able to fall asleep soon, but most likely he would fall asleep at sunrise, as usual.

Tom went out the backdoor to brush his teeth with a bottled water, spitting into a bush, stopping to stare after hearing a twig snap about ten yards into the forest, followed by another snap a few feet further, and then stillness. His bright white pallor and the raccoon-like circles around his eyes were the result of his nocturnal lifestyle. He avoided direct sunlight, restricting his daytime movement and covering the windows in his room at the apartment he shared with his sister with cardboard; he was used to looking at things in the dark. He blinked a few times after catching the movement of a possum under a thicket of trees, tugging at the shadows for other movements with his night vision, and went back inside to lay awake in the tent inside their dad's bedroom.

Brooke and Moody shared a tent, presumably because their friendship was so platonic that nothing would happen between them. As they settled into their sleeping bags Brooke nestled into Moody, pretending to do it in her sleep, and Moody put one arm around her.

Benny and Ann switched into the thermal pajamas and wool socks that they usually brought on camping trips, then settled underneath layers of comforters. Ann slept with her head tucked up under Benny's chin and he laid straight on his back with his arms crisscrossed across his chest like a mummy in its tomb. Ann felt sick from the absinthe, which, as it turned out, had not helped anyone's buzz and tasted like the cheap grappa she'd once tried at a cousin's wedding. She drifted off to sleep, quite luckily, as everyone else was too uncomfortable to get any rest.

Each creak of the airbeds would set off a series of squeaks in response, like frogs ribbiting to each other across a chain of lily pads.

Kaela and Mark talked quietly in their tent: what would her dad think about the state of the cabin, how would they get the van out of the mud in the morning, and was it such a good idea to have everyone isolated together for the weekend like this? They didn't talk about Cat, even though she was the reason for the trip; thoughts of her could cut like a rock stuck inside of a shoe, making every step forward hurt.

Just as Kaela began to fall asleep, she heard a scraping from the middle of the wall, like a talon scratching against the grain of the wood. But it didn't travel back and forth, or up and down. It dragged from right to left, over and over. Brooke heard it from her tent, too, and told herself it was something knocked loose from the wind, a small animal building a nest, the breath of the cabin itself, none of them reason enough to rouse from bed.

Tom was sitting upright inside his tent, his blankets scattered around him. He knew there was no chance that he would sleep and wanted to go outside to kill time until the morning, even if it was cold. But he didn't want to wake anyone up or give them reason to scrutinize his actions. He continued to sit and think.

Nothing could be seen from inside the tents and Kaela became aware that the window panels she had left open for fresh air made it impossible to make out any shapes looking out, but left them exposed to anyone looking in. She slid the window zipper shut to fully close them off, a sensation of being watched shooting ice up her spine. As she reached for the window above Mark, she caught sight of two wide eyes staring at her from a few feet away, then realized it was just Moody's coke bottle glasses facing in her direction, set aside for safekeeping. She let out a small, quick laugh and was jarred by the sharpness of the sound, like a bark in the middle of the night. Shielded from the creeping certainty of being watched, she pulled the blankets up to her chin and had halting half-dreams, made fragile by the croaking nighttime sounds around her.

One dream took full form, one with her friends involved in some form of choppy outing, but they were doing their own thing while she and Cat were doing another; they were together, a separate unit from the rest. The other group seemed to be having a better time, their laughs echoing across rooms and around corners, but to be with them meant leaving Cat. Leaving Cat would be an irreversible departure, while being with Cat meant doing what Cat wanted to do, for better or worse, and she could not pull herself away.

Chapter 4

Around 6 am Mark went outside for his first smoke of the day, the sound of which signaled to Tom that it was socially acceptable to stir from his tent. He headed directly to the bathroom before anyone else could slip in before him. He could feel freezing air drifting in from the single paned glass.

Kaela crawled out through her tent flap and stretched to crack her back, a wrenching sound guaranteed every time, but it felt like she was pulling something out of place and stopped, leaving her back tight and strained. The cabin was quiet, as though everyone were on the verge of getting up but were taking one more shot at sleep. Sunshine was pouring in through the windows and she went outside to show Mark how her dad had trained the chipmunks to answer to being called. She found the old tin of seeds near the door off the kitchen and stepped outside in her robe, which barely protected her from the near frost. "Chip chip chip chip," she called. "Chip chip chip chip."

Mark smiled as a couple of chipmunks darted along the edge of the woods line, brown fur skittering across crisp red leaves. The air was chilled to the point that it seemed even more fresh, like pure ozone, a metallic tang to each breath. More chipmunks began to appear, a habit they had cultivated from years of Kaela's father's training. They went quietly back inside to warm up and let the chipmunks scamper without them as a distraction.

Over the next hour the rest eventually clawed their way out from their sleeping bags and struggling into standing positions, their backs bent from contorting on the air mattresses. Once upright they began to clatter about making breakfast (scrambled eggs, bacon, vegan bacon, and vegan pancakes). The coffee maker was out of commission as a critter had chewed through the wire, so they drank Cokes instead. Afterwards they all went outside to smoke and stare at the sunken van. Kaela, Mark, and Tom looked for leverage to help unstick it from the mud but all they found were cardboard boxes they could flatten behind the wheels and a couple of shovels. "We're lucky that the ground hasn't frozen yet," said Mark. "There's probably more shovels in the tool shed, right?" He and Kaela walked to the shed, past the others squinting into the sunrise, lending an unnecessary seriousness to the scene. Tom stood at the end of the row, wearing three hoodies rather than a coat, which he forgot to pack.

"There's a hatchet stuck in the tree right about eye level, behind you, next to your head," said Benny. "I tried pulling it out but couldn't get it to budge," and with that the others converged on the tree, each giving the rustic Excalibur a pull, keeping them occupied for a few minutes.

Kaela and Mark grunted as they neared the shed when they saw the lock hanging on its hinge. The door creaked open with a metallic groan as it swept a pile of leaves further inside. They could see a collection of rusted bikes, half-full bags of charcoal, spare lumber, a rake, a snow shovel, and a couple of regular shovels, which looked to have been the only two tools purchased within the past decade.

"What's all that?" asked Mark, nodding his head towards the back of the shed. There was a design repeatedly etched across the wall, of a square containing a triangle which then contained another square and triangle, until the artist could not make them any smaller. There was also a message covered over with black splotches, only the edges of the letters visible from behind the ink.

"Oh geez. It looks like we have an infestation of teenagers hanging out around the cabin while we're gone. Like a party spot. How would they ever even find this place?" asked Kaela, exhausted by the very idea.

"Maybe Dad had some of his students out here a few times and they came back out on their own," said Tom, who had crept up behind them and was looking in over their shoulders.

"No, that doesn't make sense. If they were in college they would have their own spots to meet up. This had to be teenagers."

"Maybe someone built a place close by the cabin and you guys just didn't realize it," said Mark. "Maybe they have kids that need a place to sneak out for a little debauchery."

"I don't like this. They might have caused more damage that we haven't seen yet. Tom, make yourself useful and walk around the cabin – see if there's anything else, like graffiti."

Mark tried and failed not to smirk as Tom walked away and they carried the shovels back with them. Kaela said "It's probably best not to tell everyone else about this, it might freak them out."

"*Why?*" Mark asked, his voice overtly nasal with irritation. "Cat would have told them. We should tell them, even just because it's funny. You worry too much about what people are thinking."

"I do not, this is a legitimately weird situation already and I don't want anyone to worry more than they already are. It isn't funny that someone has been coming here without permission, doing God knows what inside the house… The mattresses. Was it teenagers peeing on the mattresses? AND SHITTING ON THE COUCH!?"

"Jesus H. Christ, teenagers didn't shit on the couch. It would have been way bigger. It was skunk-sized at best."

Altogether, save for Tom taking his sweet time walking the perimeter of the property, Benny and Moody were given the first shift with the shovels. "Get to digging boys, my turn for a smoke break," said Mark. The others stood around awkwardly in case they needed to take a turn digging, turning over topics at random to keep from watching in silence. But they were tired and, with Coke being a poor substitute for coffee, they quickly ran out of things to say, leaving them in the dull silence they had attempted to avoid.

In a move of conversational altruism, Ann offered, "While we're all here, my turn to tell a story." Relieved, nobody argued with her.

"I don't have any made-up stories for you, but I do have a story about something that really happened to me once. My best friend in my hometown is Lauren, she still lives there actually, working at the movie theater we both worked at in high school. That was my first job. We were at each other's houses all the time and on the last day of fifth grade I went to her house to stay the night. But at first, she said for us to go for a bike ride around her neighborhood because her parents had someone coming over and we were supposed to stay away until they were gone.

"What was happening was Lauren had an older sister named Courtney that had bone cancer, but she had been doing well for years, she looked so healthy, and then the cancer came back and she got very sick very fast. She went through chemotherapy and radiation but they also had alternative healers try to help. They even made a thousand paper cranes to wish the cancer away. And this time they had a new kind of healer over, so we were supposed to give them space.

"But we were getting bit up by mosquitos even as we rode our bikes. I can still remember the sight of the backs of Lauren's legs covered in mosquitos while she tried to pedal faster to get them off. Finally, we couldn't take it anymore and went inside the house even though they still had someone over. We tried to sneak by to Lauren's room but her family was all sitting in the living room and asked us to stay. They were talking to two people that also said that it was okay for us to be there and that it would be good to have 'young spirits present.'

"After a few minutes the healer smudged each of us, and when it was my turn it felt like a warm wind blowing against my body and she was like 'feel different?' I think it was because my parents' divorce was right around that time. She must have been able to sense that something was wrong. The guy that she had brought with her was playing the drums the entire time, they were like bongo drums and she had him follow her around as she performed a ceremony throughout the house to get rid of any dark spirits. The way she put it was she was letting them know that they were not welcome and that it was time to move on.

"We were all really quiet so we could listen to her as she moved through the house. But before she got started Lauren's mom asked if the healer wanted to know any areas they thought needed attention and she was quick to stop them, like 'no, I need to pay equal attention to all areas, it's best not to tell me places to focus on.' During the ceremony she sang a song in another language and walked through the entire house. When she came back to the living room she seemed a little tired out and Lauren's mom asked if she found anything. Now, before this visit, we had all always talked about how there was this one window with a tall bush outside of it that blocked out most light, and it always felt like someone was outside, hiding between the bush and the window. Like someone watching us from within the leaves. Sometimes we would dare each other to stand with our backs up against the window and see how long we could last, but it would give us such a shiver up the spine that we'd jump away. Usually we tried not to go near it.

"And there was this area in the basement that really freaked us out. They had a pool table downstairs that we would play with, basically knocking the balls around with our hands, but the other half of the basement was the laundry room. They hung up sheets across the middle of the basement to create a divider but it made it super creepy, like someone was standing just on the other side of the sheets, listening to us. Even if one of her parents went back there to run a wash it felt like there was someone else over there, the sensation never went away. But like I said, nobody told the healer about these spots beforehand.

"After Lauren's mom asked about it the healer said that she had found two dark spirits, one in front of the window by the back bedroom and another in the basement, near the laundry machines. Also, they had a dog, this huge Samoyed named Whitney, and she would never go down to the basement. We would go down there all the time and call her to us, because if she came down it would make us feel safer, but she would always stop at the top step and refuse to come any further. Lauren asked if animals can sometimes sense spirits and the healer said they can and that they shouldn't be surprised if the dog was suddenly willing to go into the basement. After they left, Lauren went downstairs right away and called for Whitney and she went down, no problem. From that day forward that dog never had a problem with going into the basement again. And all of that has contributed to my world view. It proved to me that there is an afterlife."

"The thing is, it doesn't prove anything to the rest of us, because all we have is your word for it," said Moody, uncharacteristically morose. "And doesn't it seem likely that you remembered there being scary spots *after* she told you there were ghosts there?"

"My telling you should be enough," said Ann, offended by the insinuation.

Tom sidled up quietly, perched on a log stump circling the fire pit and changed the topic. "Well, I did notice one other thing that wasn't here before. It must be something Dad was working on."

"What?" asked Kaela.

"There are a ton of carved wooden mushrooms going back into the woods. Like, someone sat and carved them out of wood, then set them up, going back about twenty yards."

Everyone went to look, Benny striking his shovel face first into the mud like a professional digger. There were dozens of mushrooms nestled in the woods behind the cabin, scattered about, some half-hidden by the leaves. They were charming, crouched so low they barely stood above the downed logs and foliage.

"It must've been your dad," said Brooke. "I mean, it's got to get pretty boring up here all alone, right?"

"He was never alone for long," said Tom.

They walked around, taking in the mushroom carvings, while Mark and Kaela took a turn trying to uproot the van from the muck. Once some progress had been made (which was hard to judge considering mud's tendency to ooze every which way), they placed the car mats under the front tires and covered the ground with dry leaves to create traction. Then the group tried to push it out from the rear while Kaela timed bursts of acceleration for each forward push. Rather than dislodging, the wheel seemed to sink in even further, spraying thick chunks of mud at everyone as they pushed. They shouted to her to quit driving as the van set in deeper and then they stood there, hands-on-hips, as it became clear that they were going to need outside help.

"Let's give it a day before we try to flag anyone down. Maybe it will even dry up on its own, that's all we need to happen. Then we could drive right out of this easy," said Kaela as she dismounted from the driver's seat. "And to be honest, it's unlikely that we'll find many people around to help. Most people don't live up here year-round and most of the summer people are gone by the first week of October."

Sweating despite the cold, Benny said "Screw it. Let's go for a walk. Maybe we'll be able to get a signal from somewhere else or spot a hunter or fisher to flag down – if anyone is around, that's who it would be."

As she watched the rest rub and stomp the mud splatters off their clothing, Kaela wondered what Cat would have thought; it was hard to gauge how she would react to things. It would be considered a win so long as she wasn't bored. Guessing at her reaction was futile, only the real thing would do, and with the air of one forcing her attention back to the task at hand, "Sorry guys, I think the soil up here is mostly clay. I should have considered that when we parked. It would've been better to park alongside the cabin. Still, it's weird it sunk *this* much."

"Maybe a Dogman sat on it to make it sink," said Mark.

"This would take a pack of dogmen," said Brooke.

"Maybe he's the one that took a shit on the couch," said Benny.

Kaela smiled a little and Tom, covered in so much dirt it looked like he did it on purpose, said "It's a good idea to leave the van alone for today and take another shot at it tomorrow. We should go for a walk. We don't need to drive anywhere today, anyway."

"Yeah, plus we have plenty of brewskies," said Mark.

"And the rest of the absinthe," said Brooke.

"And the Fireball," said Moody.

It was near ten am and they went inside to fill two coolers with water, soda, beer, and snacks. They set off on the hike past the wooden mushrooms, through the thicket, to the edge of the tall overbank overlooking the lake.

"Look," said Mark, pointing. "There is a gate over there with a No Trespassing sign." They looked over and, in the distance, stood an overgrown metal fence post with a new black and white sign.

"Tom, was that always there?" asked Kaela curiously.

He looked over. "I don't think so. But maybe. We should go to the island. I can see the rowboat's still overturned next to where the dock was pulled in."

They climbed gingerly down the cliffside, slipping and laughing, underneath a bright, clear blue sky with billowing, marshmallowed clouds. The sun was beaming over the ruddy treetops and they felt like they were in their twenties again. They grabbed hold of long grasses and tree roots to stabilize themselves on their descent, finally coming to the bottom next to the beached dock.

Kaela stopped for a moment and imagined how good it would feel to swim in the lake. Crisp and pure. But it was far too cold to even consider. Instead, they boarded the rowboat in two awkward shifts and crookedly rowed the mile out to the island, their laughs echoing across the water.

The island had an embankment that they could drag the rowboat up onto, then they had to climb a steep, sandy incline of tangled, exposed pine tree roots that snarled out from the edge of the woods and then ducked back into the earth, until they reached the top, where it settled into subtler inclines and bumps, and they took in the woods, which was made up entirely of pine. The island itself jutted in all directions, with offshoots of land elbowing out rather than a curve. The ground was layered in pine needles, softening their every footstep, the groundcover swallowing their movements. It gave them a lofty feeling, like walking in a bounce house.

It was a small island, only five acres, but it was not possible to see from one side to the other through the pine thicket. They began walking around the shoreline, looking out to the lake and in at the trees. The conversation never strayed far from past camping trips, updates on mutual friends, and what they were all making for dinner that night, which was a potluck.

"All I brought is chips and stuff to make guac, I had no idea this was a big to-do," said Tom. "There's not even any other kinds of dip."

"Oh, I think there's plenty of dips up here," said Mark with a smirk.

"You know," interrupted Kaela, "I think that this is where our uncle's explosion happened." They all stopped to take in a large mound of land with a cavern in its side.

"Yeah, this was obviously been blown apart," said Moody, more impressed than he had anticipated.

"It looks like an actual cave," said Mark, walking closer. "Like a bear could come walking out."

"I did hear a big splash in the water earlier," said Benny. "Could've been a bear."

"Jesus, there's hardly any bears up here, and they're more scared of you than you are of them," said Kaela. "Come on, let's check it out, we have nothing better to do. It's only, what, like 2?" Regardless of the time, they began filing into the cavern single file. It had a narrow entry but then opened up wide enough for them to all fit inside with only Benny, Mark, and Tom having to duck their heads. They looked around, their laughing muffled by the soil as they breathed in the smell of tree roots, underground soil, insects, and other subterranean growth.

"Hey, look at this, must be a teenager hideout," said Brooke, holding a lighter to the wall behind her.

The others turned and saw rocks and cigarettes jammed sideways into the dirt at the back of the cavern. It looked to be near a hundred sharp little protrusions sticking out.

"What a weird thing for them to do," said Kaela, scrunching her face up to give the walls a look of proper scrutiny.

"Yeah," said Mark. "It's giving me the heebie-jeebies."

They filed out from the cavern, their side quest concluded, and continued walking along the lakeshore, winding their way one-by-one through the remains of the trail, which had become gnarled by sticks and fallen branches. When they got to the easternmost end of the island they stopped for a break, sitting on the ground and cracking open beers. There were no visible homes or signs of human life anywhere along the shore of the mainland, though nobody admitted to searching for either. Benny seized the lull in conversation to tell his story.

"I have one for you guys," said Benny. "This happened to me some years back, right after college. I had kept in touch with a guy I knew from high school, his name was Amir, and I needed some time to figure out my next step, and it turned out that he needed someone to sublet his room at the house he was renting. He was going overseas, I think. I didn't know him that well but I needed somewhere to go that wasn't my parents' house to gather my thoughts. This place was off-campus – well, I say off-campus but it was actually pretty far away. It was," he laughed, his eyes shutting as his face spread into a maniacal smile, "called Scumtown. There was absolutely nothing there, except for a party store run by a guy that lived above it and a church that was always hosting hootenannies. Their billboard was updated every week, you know, with the hanging letters, and they were always having a hootenanny."

"Did you ever go?" asked Ann.

"No, but we should have. There was nothing else to do around there. I think the only other business was a post office, there wasn't even a school or any restaurants. There might have been a cemetery, too. Yeah, there was one, right across from the post office. My buddy and his friends were renting this place because it cost basically nothing to live there, like $500 a month for a house split between five guys. It was perfect for people that had no money and God knows we were all broke. The only one I really knew was Amir, but he wasn't even around, he went home pretty much the entire time I was there. The other guys were fine, just gamers, really into Final Fantasy. They were always stoned. They used to watch *Jeopardy* every night and would get almost every single answer right.

"It wasn't a bad situation for a few months, a place to stay for dirt cheap. Except there was something up with that house. I wasn't there a whole lot, I spent most of my time at the bars and I pretty much only went there to sleep. But the thing was that it was impossible to sleep at this place. I couldn't put my finger on why but every time I was just about to fall asleep something would startle me awake.

"And then a lot of weird things started happening. Like lights turning on when I knew they had been turned off, the tv changing channels for no reason, and sometimes things would fall over that shouldn't have. Like a pile of books slipping sideways off a desk. I wasn't too concerned because I was ready to leave as soon as I made up my mind about where I wanted to go next but I was kind of taking my time before making a final decision. Then one night I was the only one in the house, which was the one and only time that I was ever there alone. I went to light a cigarette, this was back when I still smoked, but I couldn't find my lighter anywhere. I always kept one on top of the dresser and I had almost nothing there besides some clothes, so it was impossible to lose anything in that room. I didn't even bother clearing a drawer to keep my things in, it all fit in my luggage and I just kept storing my clothes in it.

"I went and checked around the house for a lighter, and there were always lighters all over the place because everyone smoked. But I couldn't find a single one. So, I tried to light it off the gas stove. I still don't understand what happened but when I leaned in for a light the flame turned into a baseball sized fireball and singed my fucking eyebrows off. It was the worst timing because I had a couple of job interviews lined up and all of a sudden there I was with the biggest forehead in the world. Because of that I decided to put off interviewing for even longer, until my eyebrows grew back, which took months.

"That's when I moved out to Colorado. But before I moved I talked to Amir on the phone to let him know I was leaving. He asked me if I had noticed anything strange about the house and I told him about some of the stuff I saw. He started laughing his ass off when I told him about the fireball. I asked him why he asked me about weird things happening and he said that the house was probably haunted and that they've had a lot of people come over and say they saw weird things. And then he asked me if I remembered Mike Ewer, this other guy that went to our high school.

"I hadn't seen Mike since we graduated and this was all before social media, you know, back when you had no idea what happened to people until an actual high school reunion. It turned out that Amir had moved into that house on Mike's invitation and then one night when no one else was home Mike shot himself. He was a pretty depressed guy. Amir said that ever since then there had been a ton of unexplained things happening, like flickering lights and missing objects, but they always felt like Mike was just messing with them. Like ghost pranks. Mike was still hanging out.

"I couldn't believe that Amir didn't mention that to me and he said it was because he didn't want to poison the well by telling anyone what to expect and he knew that Mike wouldn't do anything to seriously hurt people. It was kind of like visiting with an old friend without knowing that he was there."

"You guys better hope that I don't croak first or I'm going to haunt the fuck out of you," said Mark, his green eyes slitted with mirth as he pictured it.

"Who do you guys think will die the first out of us, for real?" asked Moody.

"Probably you, to be honest," said Brooke. "At this point your blood must have the same alcohol proof as moonshine."

They stood up and began dusting themselves off, mainly concerned about not setting the pine needle forest carpet on fire with any stray cigarette butts and searching for discrete places to pee before starting on the walk back. The guys each peed to the side of some bushes and the women walked up a little inland into the woods, joking about not wanting to split up but also not wanting anyone close enough to hear them pee.

Kaela went further into the pine thicket for a covert spot. She tried to focus on the sounds of the birds chirping, the squirrels shuffling, and the wind to drown out the sounds of her friends' movements. She looked around and noticed divots in the ground, spread at odd intervals. It was as if someone had been striking a shovel into the ground, lifting it, then moving on to strike it into the next spot. She began walking a little longer to see if the indentations continued further inland.

"Where are you Kae?"

"Did you fall into a large hole and need us to save you?"

She called out backwards towards them. "Come out this way, get the guys, there's something up over here."

As the rest of the group gathered and tracked her down, she pointed out the divots. "It looks like someone has been digging at random spots over here, come check this out."

"Why would someone even think to do this?" asked Ann, looking over the odd collection of holes. "If someone were out here what would they even be digging around out here for?"

"Buried treasure?" asked Brooke.

"Could an animal do this?" asked Moody.

"It seems unlikely," said Mark with a frown, crouching to stare harder at a pile of upturned earth.

"This reminds me," said Tom tentatively. "This is the right area... I think I put a time capsule around here when I was a teenager."

"Maybe someone is looking for your time capsule. Someone that really needs, I'm guessing, a retainer, mildewed baseball cards, and a letter to Future Tom?" said Ann.

Tom paused for a moment then said "Later on I'll coming back out with a shovel and look around for it. Let's start walking back to the boat."

They continued through the middle of the island rather than walking along the remainder of the shoreline, and the half-dug holes continued to appear. When they reached the center of the island they came upon a massive pile of sticks.

"It looks like someone's tree fort got knocked down," said Benny.

"Except for those two sharpened sticks," said Brooke.

There were two long branches with the ends carved to points, each like a set of fingers curled over the pile. "I think it's supposed to be horns," said Kaela. "Like goat horns."

"Look at that, you're right," said Mark.

They took a few steps back to take in the entire wooded sculpture. The short, blunt branch protruding from the back could reasonably pass for a tail and there were four branches touching the ground while the bulk sat on top, like a hollow body set over animal legs. But the figure had no face, just an emptied gap held firm by the interlocking sticks surrounding it.

Moody pretended to kick out the legs, to which they all yelled "no!" and recoiled. Disturbing the pile seemed like the type of action that would come with consequences. They stepped carefully around the pile and continued towards the boat. The dig marks gradually phased out until they disappeared altogether as they got closer to the opposite shore.

They pulled the rowboat out to the lake and hobbled onto it, careful not to tip it over. The return trip went smoothly, the surface of the lake stilled and reflecting the smokey hues of the changing sky above them, which was now overcast and interspersed with splashes of sheer blue peeking out from behind the grey. The changing position of the sun cast a long shadow from the forest, covering their sweaty crew with a surprising chill.

Once back to the cabin they began to mix drinks and start cooking, a scene turned chaotic due to high demand on the small number of cooking utensils, pans, and space. But they were relieved to be indoors as sharp drops of rain began pelting down within minute of their return.

This was of no matter to Tom, who, after gathering a few supplies, dug out one of his father's old rain ponchos from the front closet and rowed back out to the island on his own, armed with a shovel, a pickaxe, a measuring tape, and a flashlight.

Chapter 5

Kaela took a break from food prep to set up the boombox, being of the opinion that all meals are best prepared with music in the air. She tuned it to an up north radio station while they cooked, which was playing nothing but hits from the eighties. The kitchen and dining room were one and the same, both housed in a narrow stretch ten feet wide and twenty feet long, with uncurtained windows spanning along each side. There was one windowless wall at the far end of the room with a door facing the fire pit. The stove was small, only two burners and enough space in the oven for one baking tray. Brooke went outside and attempted to build a fire for roasting hotdogs, saying that was the only proper way to eat them and that she was sure the wood was still dry enough to catch. She had a few logs stacked into a tent formation and was beginning to collect kindling for the bottom when the harsh sprinkle gave way to a bona fide downpour.

"Do you think it's safe to cook hotdogs in the fireplace?" she asked speculatively, shaking the rainwater from her hair and clothes once back inside.

"Probably, is one fire really different from another?" answered Kaela. She finished cleaning off the small counter space and let Benny step in. She looked out at the rain with her lips pressed tightly together. "I wish Tom hadn't gone out alone. He's probably going to wait the rain out on the island and catch pneumonia looking for some time capsule that disintegrated years ago."

"He's a big boy, he can find his way back on his own," said Mark as he cracked open a fresh beer.

The group started to razz each other about getting in the way, hogging the counter space, and other general complaints that old friends dish out. They were each careful not to point out the disappointment of a second night spent inside the cabin rather than camping outdoors, plus the certainty of the van submerging deeper into the mud as they spoke. Finally, exhausted from avoiding the elephant in the room, they began to eye the remaining absinthe. After watering down each cup, Mark ad-libbed a toast to Cat, with one eye on Kaela to be sure he was doing it right.

"To Cat, who we all miss. She would have really enjoyed this weekend. Even camping inside and this shitty absinthe. To Cat, who always knew how to have fun." They began clinking their cups together, the sound of plastic taps, before sipping and grimacing through their portions of the absinthe.

Soon feeling warmer and fuzzier, complaints dwindled as they turned their focus to gossip about people they knew from college while they finished making dinner. Mark added more oil to the hummus while Kaela chopped carrots, red peppers, and cucumbers for dipping. Brooke hurried semi dry wood inside to feed a fire in the fireplace throughout the night, an idea nobody tried to dissuade her from. Moody set to baking brownies and loomed behind Ann and Benny as they husked corn on the cob and chopped up strawberries, grapes, oranges, and melon for fruit salad. Tom's contribution was meant to be a lime heavy guacamole, but without him there to defend the tortilla chips they started snacking on them while they worked, unanimous in their mutinous snacking.

"I brought stuff for smores, too," said Brooke. "I can set aside longer sticks for marshmallows, we could still make them inside."

"We should play *Head Trip* later, too. It's this VHS game with this creepy old guy in a cloak that tells you to do random things. It's the best," Kaela hyped.

"I'm not so great at learning new games," said Mark forebodingly.

"No, it's really easy. We played this so many times when we were kids that the tape almost wore completely out. You know how on old tapes the video would start to fade in and out? We had to copy it over to a new tape so we could keep playing. That's how good this is."

"This is going to be a shitshow," said Benny under his breath.

"No, really —" started Kaela but she was cut off by a knock on the kitchen door by the windowless wall at the same time that Tom stomped in through the front door. Disoriented by the sudden commotion from both ends of the cabin, Kaela wavered a moment before moving to open the back door. There was nobody there, only the usual side view of the fire pit. The door of the shed was slightly open and she wondered if someone had skittered quickly inside after knocking, but froze at the thought. After a beat passed she decided that they would have seen a person move past the side windows had they fled that direction. The knocking sound was likely from the cabin settling, a pressurized reaction to Tom's entrance from the other side.

The others didn't notice her confusion and Moody shifted attention back to Tom. "Did you find the time capsule, man?" he asked, creasing his face while taking in Tom's water-logged and muddied clothes.

"I found it," said Tom, with the delivery of someone trying to discourage conversation through the sheer power of monotone.

"Can we see it? Did you write any letters to your future self?"

"No. It's private. I'd rather not talk about it."

"Oh, come the fuck on Tom," laughed Ann. "Throw us a bone. Tell us what was in the capsule." The tarp crinkled as she leaned forward from the couch eagerly.

"What's in the box? *What's in the box?*" asked Benny with a corny grin, motioning to the bulk outlined by the garbage bag Tom was carrying.

Tom kept his eyes fixed against the wall and he furrowed his brow, crinkling his forehead with aggravation, as though they had been hounding him for hours. "Like I said, it's private," and he walked past them to his tent in the back room; a dragon tucking away his treasure.

"I bet he didn't find it and doesn't want to admit it," said Kaela.

"I bet it was really embarrassing pornography," said Mark.

Tom came back into the room and asked, "Where are the chips at?" to which they all smirked to each other.

"Maybe you forget to bring them?" said Benny with a straight face.

Tom didn't turn to look at him but his face soured. "No, I didn't forget to bring them."

"Are they still in the van?" asked Brooke, joining in.

Tom sighed as though heavily burdened. "No."

"Okay, Tom, we ate the chips. We got hungry and didn't think it would be a big deal to have some while we cooked. I'll buy you more chips when we get back home," said Kaela. Tom gave a curt nod and went back to his tent, to the relief of the rest.

Soon they were done making their dishes and set them out on the long table in the dining area with unwarranted formality. The variety of finger foods had been given an actual degree of presentation, making sure the dishes were centered and placing plastic cutlery atop triangled paper towels as place settings. Ann lit candles she had found in the back of a cupboard, the light in the cabin dimmed even more as the sun went down and the cloudy sky turned from grey to ink black. They took their seats and set to dinner and cocktails, their faces flushing and their stories growing more chaotic as the meal progressed, and it began to feel like a true weekend getaway. They relaxed, leaving their worries over the van for the morning.

"Good job on the food, everyone. It would've been better with some chips, but we all make mistakes," said Ann, down-turning the lefthand corner of her mouth.

Tom got a look on his face like he'd swallowed a fly and then, assuming a saintlike countenance, said nothing for a full minute, visibly brooding. Finally, he said, "You can still use the guac with the veggies."

"I have to admit something, I've been holding out on you all. I wasn't sure if I liked you guys enough to share, but-" Mark left the room and they waited for their prize. He came back in waving a thick green bottle. "There's a real bottle of absinthe. This is the good stuff. It has actual wormwood in it."

"Thanks for finally accepting us, years into knowing us, jackass," said Benny.

Mark began refilling their cups as the rain poured down over the windows. The crackle of the fire, the flickering flames of the candles, the slow drip of wax pooling into the candleholders, and the steadying warmth from food and drink settled their nerves. Bridge smiled across the table at Moody as Tom reached over and dipped a finger into the pooling red candle wax, then held it above the flame and watched it remelt. It softened and dripped back down on top of the candle wick, snuffing it out, right at the moment that something slammed into the window directly behind him. They jumped from their seats and looked outside but it was too dark to tell what they were looking out into. Whoever was out there could see them, but they could not do the same back, their eyes disoriented from looking into flames and by the waves of rain that were flooding down the windowpanes.

They turned to look at each other, not wanting to look back out into the dark rain and then began blowing out the candles and turning off the table lamps in the living room, instinctually cloaking themselves in darkness, but stopped short of snuffing out the fireplace, leaving their silhouettes still visible to anyone outside. They crowded into a nervous knot in the living room, which had two sets of windows that they quickly pulled curtains over. Trying to keep their voices low, they began furiously discussing what could have made the sound. An animal, a branch broken by the wind, something falling off the roof, or something else altogether.

"It could have been a bird flying into the side of the house," said Ann, which was answered with quick nods.

"Maybe it would be best if we take a look outside," said Moody, turning to look back into the passage to the dining room. The rest agreed that it was a good idea and looked at Moody expectantly, it being his idea.

"I'll come out, too," offered Benny, adding, "I'm not afraid to die," with a roguish smile.

They spent a miserable minute putting on their coats, finding flashlights, and then quietly slipped out the front door. The others could track their movements outside as their flashlights lit up the woods, their beams shifting direction with each step. Moody could be heard calling out "Show yourself!" and laughing as they sloshed through the rain. The rest watched them round the corner, with Brooke moving along to watch their progress past the kitchen windows. They paused outside and looked in, Brooke waving, a shadow covered in rivulets from the downpour over the windows. They continued and were momentarily out of sight until they circled back towards the front door. The rest remained in the front room, keeping an eye on both the front and the back doors, their ears alert for further sounds from the dining room. There was nothing to be heard but the sound of the water sluicing down from the roof, the outside view warped by the current of rainwater. Another minute passed without the return of the guys; a circuit around the cabin would take a minute at most unless something caught their attention.

"I'm going to go out there and see what's up," said Mark.

"They're probably trying to scare us," said Brooke, drunk and irritated.

Kaela shook her head no at Mark and he paused to reconsider. Ann grabbed a flashlight and headed for the door and he gave Kaela a look as he headed out behind her. But she stopped in the door frame and he almost walked into her. They both looked outside silently until Kaela pushed past them to see what had them frozen in place. She saw Moody and Benny next to the well, looking at her with wide eyes and frozen faces, until they broke into a run straight for the cabin. Their running sloshed water in all directions and they slammed the door behind them, crowding Ann and Mark back inside.

"We saw someone standing in the woods, over behind the kitchen," said Benny quickly.

They all moved gingerly towards the windows and tried to peek out without revealing themselves. Mark drew up alongside the wall leading towards the dining room, trying to look outside without showing himself.

"You're fucking with us," said Brooke.

"We're not," hissed an ashen faced Moody.

"You could see someone from way over at the well?"

"We thought that if someone was hiding anywhere besides the woods or the shed that it would be behind the well, or inside of it, so we walked over. When you guys opened the door we saw someone in the fucking woods, it looked like a guy."

They clustered, their backs together in a circle formation, a set of eyes on each corner. Mark came back from the hallway and said, "Look, we need to put out this fire, otherwise whoever is out there will see everything we're doing."

"Fuck it, let's get in the van and go," said Ann.

"It's *stuck*. Maybe getting even more stuck now with this rain," Kaela reminded her in a tight voice.

"Everyone needs to take a minute. It's probably one of the high school kids that's been partying here," said Tom, then adding, "It's Saturday night."

"He's probably more scared of us than we are of him," whispered Moody.

Mark began putting out the fire with bottled water, a sudden popping sound which made the rest collectively flinch.

"Why would you ever think that was a good idea?" asked Kaela. "It's just some teenager walking around and now we're going to be freezing our asses off. *There is only one space heater.*"

Mark didn't say anything, his eyes narrow and alert as he waited for his vision to adjust to the absence of the fire.

The atmosphere slowly calmed in the absence of any further surprises, and the conversation over whether to confront the thwarted teenage partier shifted into sharing stories about the hideaways they used to hang out at when they were teenagers. With the mood lightened, they were careful not to think too hard about how even a rebellious teenager would not go out walking in such an intense thunderstorm. They were also careful not to mention how if one teenager was intent enough to make their way to the cabin, then perhaps others were, too.

With the fire extinguished they could see outside more easily, however the room was smokey from the extinguished fire, combined with the fog from their breathing clouding up the windows. Their view was still muddled but at least no one could see in. The rain and darkness ensured that there was no way to spot anyone outside. The frigid rain, just above freezing, ruled out any serious search of the woods. Instead they individually eyed items that could work as weapons from inside the cabin and then Kaela subtly reinforced the curtains with blankets, claiming it was to help hold in body heat but was obviously to further block them from being seen. The threat seemingly passed, they were soon cocooned inside blankets and huddled near the space heater.

"Well, it's only 9 o'clock, what should we do other than drink?" asked Ann.

"Well, we might as well play *Head Trip* while we wait for Dogman to stick his face in the window," said Kaela.

Chapter 6

Despite the delicate return of cheer to the air, an itchy, static sense of being watched persisted from the windows. It was as though someone was spying through a corner of the curtain that they had missed, or perhaps earlier in the day someone had snuck inside and hidden inside a closet, waiting for their moment to spring out, or maybe had shimmied onto the rooftop, waiting for the chimney to cool so they could lower into the house like a spider. Their eyes continuously flitted across the shadows of the room, tracking them to be sure nothing had changed between glances. They curled up in sleeping bags and blankets on the floor, so close that they were practically in a pile, forming their own panopticon, the only thing they couldn't keep an eye on being each other. The original cinder block framework did well at retaining the heat, keeping them warm for a while longer. There was no furnace or wood burning stove, but so long as they kept clustered near the space heater, they were warm enough.

A minute passed without event and as their nerves began to settle, they got steadily more drunk, each hell bent on liquid courage in case they needed to go into aggro mode at a moment's notice. The tents pitched throughout the cabin were suddenly unsettling, each able to conceal an intruder from within or behind. Talk of the person in the woods had simmered into confidence that he was probably from the family that had put up the 'No Trespassing' sign at the edge of the property, come to check on who was at their Dad's cabin out of neighborly concern.

Relaxed, they began to complain about Mark putting out the fire. It seemed increasingly unlikely that there had actually been anyone outside and more likely that Benny and Moody got spooked by a weird looking tree trunk, mistaking a hollow for a face. Kaela finished setting up the board game and was messing with the tv to get it to play the *Head Trip* VHS tape. The tv flickered from static to black and then the deep bass of the theme song began to play, the screen a tombstone with credits rolling across it. Fog wafted across the scene while a stocky man in a hood stepped out from behind a squat grave, introducing himself as the Game Ghoul. "If you want to survive the night you will do as I say!" he warned them.

They decided to turn it into a drinking game since the rules were way too complicated to follow, only doing tasks as delegated by the Game Ghoul and drinking each time he insulted them (a shot of Fireball if he called them maggots, which was shockingly often). There was still a lingering uneasiness but the warmth from their nest and the alcohol settled them into a comforted, blank slate. *Head Trip* continued, the hooded actor reminding them that they were lazy maggots, an insult so frequent that even Moody felt like was going to be sick if it went on much longer.

Kaela was privately miserable over how the weekend had gone. It had been planned as a way for them to remember Cat together, but instead they were sloppy drunk just to make it to the morning without being bored or scared out of the minds. She wondered if she should have planned more things to do, actual activities like letting off paper lanterns by the lake in memory of Cat, and was angry with herself for not thinking ahead.

"Do we… really need to finish this game?" asked Benny. "No offense meant but I'm going to hurl if he calls us maggots one more time. And we should keep our wits about us for the teenage ninjas hiding in the woods."

"I'm tired but I don't think I could sleep even if I tried," said Ann. "I'll protect you from the teens, babe."

"We should still get some rest, even if it's just laying down with our eyes shut," said Mark, clearly angling for some peace and quiet.

They curled up together like a pile of dogs and listened to each other try to get comfortable, each movement shifting their partners like they were on a waterbed.

"This is ridiculous. I would go sleep in the van if the woods weren't full of murderers," said Moody.

Tom, laying at the edge of the pile, turned sideways and said, "I could tell you a scary story since we're all still up anyway. I haven't really had anything supernatural happen to me in real life, besides the time I smelled my mom's perfume in my room a year after she died. But I remember a good story that I read back in a college course on folklore that stayed with me. It's called *The Wendigo*. I don't remember any of the names of the people, or the places, and it won't be as scary based on memory, but I could tell it."

"Just make up some names, get on with the story," said Mark.

Tom winced but bore. "There was this guy in the 1800's with a rich dad, and he was a student at the top university in Canada at the time. He and his dad would go on hunting trips together and one year they decided to go further into the wilderness than they ever had before. Let's call them Walt and Walt Junior. Northern Canada had areas more remote than the places they usually went so they hired some people for help. One was a local they needed as a cook and to help maintain their campsite while they were out hunting, another was a French-Canadian guy that was a skilled woodsman to help them track game. They also brought along one of his dad's friends, a banker that was an experienced hunter, too. We'll call them Jesse, Saul, and Hank. They took a canoe and set off from the mainland to the islands north of Quebec territory. It's isolated up there, very quiet outside of wildlife, there weren't any settlements around, and they had supplies but had to plan how they used them carefully. They had no way of getting help or sending a message to anyone, which is what they wanted. Or at least what they thought they wanted."

Kaela let out a snort, the sound blunt against Tom's soothing monotone. "It sounds like me. I always say how I'd like to live up here but just imagine it. One of you would come to see me and I'd turn around and the whole front of my body would be covered in chipmunks and birds."

Tom looked at her, his exhaustion showing. "Don't interrupt. Know what? If no one is going to listen when I tell a story let's all just sit here and stare at each other in the dark in silence."

"Okay, okay, *chill* people, I want to see where this is headed," said Benny. "Please continue."

Tom lit a cigarette indoors, antagonizing everyone in one fell swoop, but no one said a thing because they secretly wanted to hear where his story was going. "They got to the edge of the mainland and they had to take canoes out the next day to reach the islands that were off the coast. Saul knew of an island that was supposed to have a ton of elk but it would take hours to canoe there and they had to wait for the next morning. For that first night they set up camp while Jesse caught fish for dinner. They were telling stories around the fire and then out of nowhere the whole woods went quiet. All of the birds, the insects, even the bats, were silent, like they were the only ones there, and then this rotten stench spread through their camp. No one could figure out what caused it, it was like spoiled milk mixed with sulfur. They started looking around for where it was coming from and it got stronger as they walked closer to the edge of the forest behind the campsite. Then the smell went away as fast as it had come and they lost track of the source. As soon as the smell was gone the animals started making sounds again, so they shrugged it off and went to sleep in their tents.

"The main point of the trip was for the younger guy, the student, to shoot an elk and bring home the antlers as a trophy, so the next day Saul, the French Canadian, took Walt Jr. out to a remote island that he had heard rumors about having a lot of elk. It took a few hours by canoe to get there and it looked as though they would probably have enough to do to make staying the night worthwhile, so while Walt Jr. set up camp Saul went to scout out the area for any signs of elk. Tracks, antler marks on the trees, things that trackers look for. While he was gone Walt kept the fire going and a few hours went by. Then Saul came back and said he hadn't seen signs of anything but he was positive they would the next day. Maybe they had been driven to the other side of the island for whatever reason.

"When it got dark, Saul and Walt Jr. started having some drinks and singing songs, passing time like people did back then. Then that same disgusting smell from the night before took over the camp, like dead fish and brine. They started heaving from the stench and then they both saw an outline of a shadow in the woods, something really tall, standing stock still and looking in their direction. They stared at it, not knowing if it was an animal or not, and then it disappeared without a sound. The smell went away with it and they rushed into their tent for the night. Neither of them wanted to talk about what they had seen, like saying what happened out loud would draw it back to them.

"They were physically spent and fell asleep even though they were pretty disturbed. Halfway through the night, Walt Jr. woke up and at first, he was confused about where he was, and as he looked around to gather his bearings he saw that Saul had fallen asleep with his feet hanging outside of the tent. We're talking about an island in Northern Canada so it was freezing outside and he couldn't let the other guy sleep like that. He woke Saul up and he was freaked out, saying he was an experienced woodsman and of course there was no way he would sleep with his bare feet hanging outside. He accused Walt Jr. of trying to pull some kind of prank and they tried to go back to sleep, but Walt Jr. could hear Saul crying to himself. He tried to act like he couldn't hear but he listened to the other guy crying for the rest of the night as well as for anything approaching from the outside.

"When the sun was almost up the woods were completely quiet but it was hard to tell if it was because the birds weren't up or if they were being quiet on purpose, and then something started croaking from up above the tent, it sounded kind of like a crow. There was this voice calling 'Saul, Saul!' Saul jumped up and ran straight out of the tent, looking to see who was calling, but there was nobody around. The voice started calling 'Saul!' out again, this time from the forest and he bolted after it. Walt Jr. gave it a couple of minutes, thinking that Saul would come back on his own, but then so much time went by without hearing the voice or Saul that he had to go make sure he was okay. There was no time for him to go back to the other camp to get help so he grabbed a gun and took off to track the guide.

"There were a lot of hard to miss signs of where Saul had been, like he'd been leaving a trail on purpose: broken branches, footprints stomped deep into mud, torn leaves. After about an hour of tracking, Walt Jr. noticed a second pair of tracks, but these looked more like elk prints. The thing is, the further he got into the forest, the more the two sets of tracks began to sync up, like they were walking together. And then the tracks began to span further and further apart, to the point that he couldn't believe what he was seeing. We're talking like fifteen feet between tracks. Then, all of a sudden there weren't any more tracks to follow. He circled further and further out from the last set but found nothing, and then he heard moaning coming from above him and looked up. Way up high in a tree there was a body splayed across a tree branch that had to be Saul, and then a shadow passed across the treetops and the body was gone.

"At this point Walt Jr. realized he was in over his head and had to canoe back to get help or else he was going to be alone on that island for another night, along with Saul and whatever had taken him. He managed to find his way back to the first camp but it took him even longer than the trip there, what with him being the only one rowing. By time he got back to the first camp he was exhausted. But once he was there, he didn't want to sound like he had abandoned their guide or that he was making any of it up, so he left it that the French-Canadian had seen a huge elk in the woods, pursued it without bothering to wait for him, that he was unable to find their friend even after searching for hours, and therefore a rescue mission was in order.

"It being almost sundown, they decided to wait until the morning to go back, so they all tried to rest up and get an early start. The other guys weren't too worried because Walt Jr. had downplayed the situation and Saul was the best woodsman out of all of them, plus the other camp and supplies were there whenever he managed to find his way back to the tent, so they weren't in any kind of panic to find him. The next morning, they canoed back over to the island but left Jesse behind to keep watch over the first camp. When they got to the second camp they found no signs of life at the tent and there hadn't been a fresh fire, so they immediately set out to retrace the trail that Walt Jr. had followed the day before. The two other guys were just as bewildered by the strange track marks and also couldn't figure out which direction to go when the tracks ran out. After a while Walt Jr. began to feel less irrational and told them everything that he had left out, and both his dad and his dad's friend kind of half believed him, half thought he'd had a psychotic break.

"They continued to look for tracks throughout the forest, because it isn't like they had a better explanation to offer. Saul could not have just disappeared into thin air; he was there, on that island, somewhere. It would be over a week before they could bring anyone else out to help look and by then the guy would probably be dead, meaning that, in a worst-case scenario, they had to at least locate his body before they left. They looked all day and finally were about to give up when they heard a human scream in the distance, saying 'My feet are burning!' and the sound seemed to be coming from up above the trees. They tried to chase it down but couldn't catch up.

"It went on and on until it was getting dark, like something was trying to keep them there, but then the screaming sounds stopped suddenly. Without that to follow they had no idea what to do next. They decided to try and camp at the second campsite for the night but when they got back to it, Saul was already there. He was standing next to the tent with a dazed look and they asked him where he had been and how he got away from whatever had him but he didn't respond; he just looked around terrified like something would come and snatch him up any second.

"He seemed to be in shock and barely said a word on the canoe trip back to the first camp, which they did in the middle of the night to get the fuck away from whatever was on that island. They could barely see where they were going but they could follow the smoke from the fire at the first camp. When they got back they all tried to act normal. They were way too tired to pack up and start the return trip, and it's not like they had any way to call for help, so they *had* to act like things were okay and rest. But they were all keeping an eye on Saul. He was extremely nervous and still had nothing to say about what had happened or where he had been, and finally Walt Sr. snapped. He started yelling at Saul, saying that he didn't even believe he was really Saul and demanded that he explain himself.

"Saul started crying and looking back towards the woods like a scared little kid. He still didn't say anything but he raised his pant leg and lifted his feet up for them all to see. The bottoms were rubbed raw with layers of skin missing from tons of friction. It was like they'd been run clean off. The next day they packed up and started home; they were like 'screw it, let's get out of here.' But even on the long trip back, Saul kept shrinking back if anyone talked to him and looking behind them to see if they were being followed. It seemed to get worse and worse and then a few weeks later he dropped dead."

"What a hoser," said Kaela, and Mark laughed.

Tom's eyes were in a stoned glaze, making it hard to tell if the death stare he was giving them was joking or serious.

"Are you guys ready for mine?" asked Mark with a crooked grin.

"You'll never have a more captive audience than right now, go for it, man," said Moody.

Tom took a drink and stared reflectively at the can, mumbling something disparaging under his breath.

Mark looked into the distance, seemingly oblivious to Tom's brooding. He started his story carefully, as though considering how to begin a confession.

"When I was in my twenties I had terrible sleep and was usually up most nights. Well, I still do that. At the time I was living at home, trying to save up some money to get my own place, and my bedroom was at ground level, as in the window was level with the grass. If you reached outside you could step up onto the yard. It was perfect for sneaking in and out when I was a teenager. It also gave a good view of stuff going on outside, like if people or animals crossed by the yard I would always notice. Even if the blinds were drawn, shadows would move across the room, there was no missing them. But my parents' house is way out in the boonies and there wasn't much traffic, which made any activity outside stand out even more. By activity I mean stuff like people going for walks or riding their bikes around, sometimes horseback riders.

"When my internet business started taking off, I would stay up through the entire night working, staying up until dawn most of the time, and sometimes I would catch weird things happening when everyone else was asleep. Like people walking by in the middle of the night, and like I said, this was out in the country. This was on a dirt road, there aren't even any sidewalks out there. There wasn't any reason to be outside at night unless you were up to some debauchery. Sometimes I would even catch these flashing lights out of the corner of my eye but whenever I looked outside there was nothing there and I figured, whatever, maybe I was imagining it, I'd been staying up too long–"

"And robo-tripping for days," added Tom.

Mark looked at him in surprise which quickly settled into mild offense, tempered by a look of labored stoicism.

"What's robo-tripping?" asked Ann.

"Forget it. It's nothing," said Mark sharply. "Now my story-telling is all fucked up."

"I'm sorry, just a bad joke," said Tom distantly.

Mark continued as though creating a diversion. "Anyway, one night I decided that I needed a break and I tried to lay down. My mind was moving too fast to actually sleep but I thought it was worth trying. I laid there for a couple hours and then around 3 am I heard this sound, like a click, and I opened my eyes. There was this light filtering through my blinds, this bright pink and purple light. I didn't turn my head to look out the blinds because I wanted whatever it was to think I was still asleep. I laid there for a few minutes and the lights kept turning and blinking, casting light rays over the walls. Eventually I tried to turn my head really slowly to get a direct look through the blinds, but as soon as I started moving it fell back and disappeared.

"When I say that I mean, it isn't like the light went out, like someone flicking a switch. It went out like something repelling backwards and then up, super fucking fast. I know you all think I'm bullshitting you, but I think it was a UFO. They came to abduct me since I'm such a perfect specimen but decided to let me age a little bit more first. Like a fine wine."

"If you consider year old Boone's Farm vintage, sure, you're like a fine wine," muttered Tom.

Mark took a sip of his Coors Light and chuckled, "Fuck you, Tom," his laugh rendered metallic through the raised can.

Tom smiled tightly and gave a long sigh, tightening his folded arms and staring towards the back hall.

Kaela made a rapid attempt to redirect the conversation and asked Mark for more details. "Are you sure it wasn't that car you kept seeing drive by?"

"What car?" Mark snapped, as though he had been through enough.

"You know, the one you kept seeing drive by, so you called a friend over for back-up…?"

"Oh, yeah. Ha. Haha! Okay, since you all like having a laugh at me, have some fun with this one. I had trouble sleeping back in high school, too. I guess I've always been kind of an insomniac, and I was living in that ground floor room–"

"Isn't that where you live now? In your parents' basement?" asked Tom.

"... Yeah. Well, like you wouldn't be living at home if your dad would let you," said Mark. Tom's face soured even more and Mark doggedly forged ahead with his storytelling. "There was this car that I kept seeing going by our house for like a week straight. It would drive by before sunrise, like 4 or 5 am, stop for a minute, and then slowly drive away. At that time everyone was toilet papering each other's houses and I was convinced that someone was planning to hit ours. And I had toilet papered so many houses that I was sure someone was out for revenge. I decided to get to the bottom of it and told a buddy of mine about the car and he stayed over the next night so we could watch for it together. Sure as shit, around five in the morning we saw headlights pulling up. We ran out and jumped into my car and took off to chase whoever it was down.

"My parents' driveway is long so it took a few seconds to get going and the other car took off. But then it stopped right as we turned out and I said 'hold on, he's gonna try something' but then the car started driving again. We took off after it but then it stopped short again. Then my friend was like 'he's reaching for something' and I almost shit myself, thinking it was a weapon like a gun or a baseball bat and this person was about to come mess us up for following him, but then the car drove away again. And then we realized that it was the newspaper delivery guy. He was stopping to reach for newspapers. That poor s.o.b. had to be terrified, like 'what the is with these country bumpkins?'"

Everyone laughed except for Tom, who had become so disgusted that he couldn't hold it in any longer. A tremor of unease began to gain traction across the group, like a small bell set off ringing louder and louder, and after a few minutes they all agreed that it was time to try to get some sleep. Whether or not they were actually tired, it was necessary to at least pretend at sleeping; they were tired of talking to each other. The conversational well had run dry.

Kaela settled into her sleeping bag and closed her eyes, thinking of how she'd like to pack up and drive home right then. Given that this was not possible, she began to wonder at how Cat would have maneuvered the night, which then gave way to thoughts of the van sinking deeper into the muck with each added minute of rain. The odd stirrings coming from within the cabin the walls no longer drew her notice, and whatever animals were living there had adjusted to the human huddle in the living room. A critter scurrying past didn't even change direction when Moody unknowingly kicked his shoes off into its path.

The rain continued until near 4 am but the sun wouldn't rise for a few more hours. Members of the group slowly fell asleep, with the exception of both Tom and Mark, each still keeping watch for odd movements from inside or out. Their eyes completely adjusted to the dark, it become unavoidable to acknowledge that they were both still awake.

"Do you think that asshole is still out there?" asked Tom, squinting his eyes at a curtained window.

"It's just some kid fucking around," said Mark.

"But where would he even come from? It must have been my dad that put those 'No Trespassing' signs up, we would have heard if someone was building a house anywhere near here. Not to mention our dad would have mentioned new neighbors when we said we were coming up here."

"The signs were posted facing this direction. Someone lives on the other side of that gate. Your dad is barely ever in Michigan, how would he even know?" Mark lit a cigarette, the click of the lighter punctuating his sentence.

"Nice," said Tom. "Tactful as always."

Mark set his jaw and exhaled. "Look, I'm not trying to be a dick, he just lives in Arizona now. It's hard for him to get up here often is all I'm saying."

"Put that out," hissed Tom.

"Don't be a dick. Plus, didn't you light up inside earlier? Don't be hypocritical."

"That was when everyone was awake, not when they're asleep. No one can stop themselves from breathing in your smoke. Take it outside. Unless you're scared to go out there?"

"I don't want to wake people up opening the door. I'll just have this one and then stop. Is that okay with you?"

"Typical," said Tom. "Typical behavior from you."

Mark stared towards Tom across the dark room. "Look, to be honest, maybe I am a little freaked out about going outside."

Tom got up from his sleeping bag and stood by the door. "I'll go outside with you."

The door groaned as they stepped outside through the front door into a dense mist, an aftereffect of the rain and near freezing temperature. They couldn't see beyond six feet in front of their faces, the van reduced to a dim outline a few yards away. "Hurry up and smoke," said Tom. Mark smirked, took a long drag, and blew in Tom's direction, the smoke congealing with the surrounding fog.

Tom stopped and looked at Mark without any expression on his face, deciding what to do, then pushed Mark experimentally. Mark's balance was thrown off and he stepped back in surprise, the back of his head knocking back into the heavy cabin door. He froze, looking over Tom's face quizzically, then moved at him fast, trying to knock him over. Tom reacted quickly, as though he had been picturing such a scenario unfolding and tried to grab Mark into a sleeper hold. Mark began to make a sound between a moan and a yell as he struggled from Tom's grip, the commotion waking the rest of the group.

When they opened the door Tom's ghostly pallor made it look like the man from the woods was attacking Mark. A half-asleep Moody reacted without hesitation, throwing the thick empty bottle of absinthe directly at Tom's head. It made a hard, cracking sound rather than breaking and Tom's grasp went limp, his face contorted in blind anger. Mark remained on the ground, curled in a fetal position, crying quietly. Chaos broke out as the group recognized Tom and tried to figure out what had happened, but Tom stood up without a word and walked into the woods. Kaela sat next to Mark, stroked his hair, repeating that everything was okay until he stopped crying and stood back up.

Benny and Ann ran after Tom to the tree line behind the house calling for him to come back. He was walking in the direction of the cliffside and without turning said loudly, "I'm going to see if there's anyone hiding out on the island," right as he tripped on one of the wooden mushrooms. The fall stunned him a minute, giving them a chance to catch up.

"You can't go out over there by yourself. It's freezing out on the lake and we're all still a little drunk. We were only asleep for like an hour," said Ann reasonably.

Tom gathered himself, got up, and continued to walk away. The couple listened to the twigs snapping under his receding footfalls and gave each other a shrug before walking back to the cabin, Tom an apparent lost cause.

Everyone agreed it was for the best that Tom wasn't in the cabin while things simmered down. Kaela and Mark went inside their tent as she privately consoled him. Benny busied himself by making everyone Bloody Mary's with vegetable garnishes he had pickled himself (asparagus, beets, cucumber, peppers, peaches). It was his surprise contribution to the weekend, meant to be a Sunday morning surprise. It was still pre-sunrise, so no one felt much like breakfast, but the drinks were welcome, and they all agreed that if you used enough garnishes it counted as a meal.

The discussion over what happened turned up little explanation in Tom's absence and Mark rendered morose and sullen. Conversation turned to the need to start back as soon as the fog lifted. They discussed ways to dislodge the vans wheels from the mud, especially considering that nobody knew if it were going to rain more or, worse, drop below freezing. Another night there could mean dealing with frozen ground, making it even more difficult to uproot the wheels. They began to gather their belongings to kill time until they had visibility, eager to load up their stuff as soon as they had the van uprooted.

After a couple of hours of painful boredom, the fog lifted and they converged outside. They considered the van, which was now knee-deep in a quagmire of thick mud. The van was parked facing the forest which left them with very little room to move forward, so their first strategic move was to place a couple of rotting two by fours they found behind the shed under the tires and reverse the van across the planks; it did little more than nearly splinter the lumber from the pressure. The warmth from the Bloody Mary's numbed them from the chill in the air, yet they kept glancing around, a tingling sensation of being watched still present through the remaining whisps of cloud.

Next they began rocking and pushing it from side to side, desperation setting in. "Some of the dried mud is crumbling off—" started Benny but he was interrupted by the sound of rapid footsteps snapping through the brush. Their faces went pale and they peered around the van to see what was coming their way, their feet sinking into the mud under their weight like quicksand, and they were relieved to see it was only Tom. He came around the other side of the cabin, held his arms above his head waving to get their attention and announced, "The island is on fire." He motioned for them to follow and they filed after him into the woods, deserting the van and rushing past the wooden mushrooms to the cliffside. Smoke was rising from the island.

"What the hell?" said Kaela in disbelief. "How could it be on fire? A lightning strike?"

"I was over there, I tried to find the source to put it out, but the smoke is coming out from underground, mostly on the far side. Something must have lit the pine needles. The bottoms of the tree trunks are turning black," said Tom. "It's spreading fast."

"We need to get help. Do they even have a fire department up here?" asked Ann.

"Maybe the lake will put the fire out? Or is there more rain coming?" added Brooke.

"It's going to kill all the trees from the roots up," said Kaela.

"It doesn't make sense, the rain should have made any kind of fire impossible. Unless it started before the rain?" said Mark, frowning.

"Whatever caused it, animals living out there are going to die. And our Dad is going to be pissed if we burn down his island. We need to start walking to that party store to get help. Plus, we need someone to help us get the van out. Sorry guys, it's a long walk but we have no other choice at this point," said Kaela miserably.

They turned from the smoking island and started walking back to the cabin to grab essentials and put on more layers for the trek. Any leftover anxiety over a person in the woods was eclipsed by the need to get help. As they gathered their supplies together there was a knock at the door. Not too loud but loud enough to be heard, a polite announcement of arrival. They stopped and looked at each other, the air turned prickly and tense, like any movement could get them stung. Mark walked to the window and looked out from the side of the curtain and turned back, ashen faced. "Benny, Moody, get over here. Is this the guy you saw in the woods?"

They moved over quietly to look past the curtain. "It could be," whispered Benny.

The man knocked again, as gently as before.

"I'm going to talk to him," announced Mark, his eyes wide, the same look he got on his face before going all-in on a game of poker, and he opened the door.

Chapter 7

"Hello? Yes? What is it?" said Mark, making his voice sound hostile to mask his panic.

A moon-faced man looked at Mark with concern. Mark wedged his right foot behind the door to obstruct it from being forced open, but the man made no movement to push it open. He didn't move at all, looking pensively at Mark as drops of condensation gathered on the lenses of his wire-rimmed glasses. The rest crowded near the door, a human wall blocking entrance.

The man clicked his tongue as though about to speak, then paused, seemingly reconsidering his approach, allowing them a few moments to look him over. On closer examination, his complexion was more pink than pale, his high forehead and slight chin flat set against his flushed cheeks and nose. His hair was overgrown into a slight shag, making its red undertone more glaring. His eyes were beady behind his glasses and they lay steadily on Mark, as though refusing to look at the rest of the group. He was soaking wet from both rain and sweat, and his waterlogged pea coat and black jeans made him look like a half-drowned sailor. His hands were in his pockets, positioned as though he were holding something, and whether or not he had a weapon with him, it made him seem unstable. He had the look of a crouched spider, full of patience and venom.

Mark began to feel increasing waves of unease and was about to slam the door back shut when the man said quickly, "Please don't be alarmed, I need some help, and I think maybe I could help you, too." He gestured towards the van.

"What can we help you with?" snapped Mark, as though the man were interrupting them during breakfast.

The man raised his hands placatingly and spoke in a light voice, carefully enunciating each word. "I mean no harm, but I'm hoping for your help figuring something out. This might sound strange but I buried something out here a while ago and I don't remember exactly where I put it. I drove all the way up here to look for it and I've been waiting for you all to leave before I started digging again. The thing is, and here is where I could really use a hand, there is a snowstorm starting later today. The ground is probably going to freeze up and this is buried kind of deep. The sooner we get started the better. Then, when we're done, I know a trick to get your van up from that ditch."

Mark turned back to look at the group but was careful to keep one eye on the visitor. "We'd like to help you, and we could definitely use the help, but I don't know." Ann gave him a frown. "Also, I hate to ask this, but I have to."

"Go on," said the man lightly.

"We've been seeing someone around the property, at night-" Mark trailed off in the hopes the stranger would step in.

"Yeah... yeah, sorry about that. Don't get upset, but once I heard about the snowstorm coming I was hoping to scare you away to get a sooner start on the dig. And, to be honest, I was curious about you. What are the chances of us all being out here at the same time?" he chuckled, with his hand still pressed hard into his coat pocket.

"Where did you park your car?" asked Mark suddenly.

"It's up along the road, tucked in past the end of the driveway."

"Wait, first what did you bury? What would we be looking for" asked Ann, stepping closer to the door.

The man peered into the shadows inside the cabin but when he answered his eyes resettled on Mark's. "To be honest, I've been up here a few times when no one else was, trying to find the right spot. I know my way around. If you guys would rather not help, I could dig on my own, but then I have no reason to help you. This is a quid pro quo. You scratch my back, I'll scratch yours."

"But what is it you're looking for?" asked Brooke.

The man pursed his lips primly and said, "This is kind of a private thing, I don't need anyone's help handling it, I just need help finding where it is."

Benny cut in. "If your car is here could one of us borrow it to run up to town? We need to call the fire department, there's an island on fire out on the lake and we can't call anyone or get help from here."

The man considered. "Your phones aren't getting a signal?"

"Is yours?" asked Benny.

The man responded curtly, "Mine neither. But if I lent you the car then there's no guarantee that you'll help me. And I don't know you well enough to trust you with my car."

"No," said Kaela, stepping behind Mark and talking over his shoulder, "We need to get help out here first, the entire island could be destroyed unless we get out of here fast. The longer we wait, the more damage is done. How about just one of us borrows your car while the rest of us stay to help?"

The man set his jaw, which made his lower lip stick out petulantly. "No. It's my car and unless you're the type of people to try and steal my car you're going to help me search. Really, the longer we talk about this the longer it'll take to get help – this is on you guys."

"Well, we need to talk this over. Do you mind waiting here a minute?" said Mark as he shut the door, to the man's annoyed chagrin.

"I can't believe you just shut the door on his face," said Brooke.

Marks hands were shaking. "That guy is obviously fucking insane. What are we doing? This thing could be buried anywhere and whatever it is is probably something batshit crazy."

"Like a mannequin in a prom dress," said Ann.

Mark pointed at her emphatically. "Exactly."

"Okay, Brooke and Moody, could you two should sneak out the back door and start walking to town? We'll keep him distracted near the firepit and help him dig," said Kaela.

"But isn't he going to notice that we're gone?" said Brooke.

"What's he going to do? Chase you down? He seems harmless. Unstable but not violent."

"Then why is he pretending to have a gun in his pocket?" asked Tom calmly.

"Maybe it's a boner," said Moody and everyone glared at him.

"Try to flag down any cars that drive by. All we need is to borrow a phone, but if they don't have a signal, then try to get a ride up to the party store." advised Kaela.

"We'll go, but if you guys manage to get his car or get the van free, come pick us up. Oh, and make sure he isn't tricking you all into digging your own mass grave," said Moody as they snuck out the back, shutting the door quietly behind them.

Chapter 8

"He makes a good point," said Ann, looking out the side window at the man. He was staring into the woods, his backed turned towards them. "Maybe we should choose a safe word to use in case anyone feels like he's about to serial kill us all."

"How about 'MURDERER' for a safe word? Also, why did those two get their lives spared? If anyone here deserves to die it's Moody," said Benny.

Tom watched Brooke and Moody's unhurried escape through the woods, made slower by their tiptoeing through the brush. Once the trees swallowed them up from sight he said, "Let's get this over with. I left the good shovel in the green shed when I got back-"

"What do we do if this guy's buried treasure turns out to be a body?" asked Ann.

"That would be great, because then we could steal his car and not even feel bad about it," said Benny.

"And I think there are extra shovels in the other shed that we could use, they're kind of old so wear gloves to keep your hands from rubbing raw," finished Tom.

They stepped outside and the man turned to them. "Well?"

"We'll help you out as long as you promise to help us later, but if your trick doesn't work to get the van out, then at least give us a ride into town."

"Deal. Let's get started then. Call me Tad, by the way. I think the most likely spot, the one area I haven't checked out yet, is in the back near the generator."

They took turns digging, working from corners into one larger hole, with Tad seeming to relish supervising their work and only occasionally helping, claiming to tire easily. He leaned against a young elm tree, bending it sideways as he watched them. "You know, I'm actually happy that you all wound up being here this weekend," he said, smiling at Ann.

She scowled at him and asked, "How deep is this thing?"

"A couple feet more, I'm positive this is the area," he said, switching to a professional tone, his smile gone and his eyes glistening. "Just curious, when are your other friends coming to join us?"

The group looked at each other furtively, no story settled on ahead of time. "They aren't feeling well. Hungover," said Kaela experimentally.

Tad frowned and shifted his weight onto his right foot, allowing the tree to settle back into standing position, then took a long sigh as he looked over the cabin as though disappointed in their work ethic. His sullenness made him seem like less of a threat and more like a spoiled child, but even when his hands left his coat pockets the hard bulk remained. Another motivator took form in the coil of smoke billowing from the island, a black snake growing longer and fuller by the minute. With the first flakes of snow beginning to fall, Mark ventured a new angle. "It seems like, at this point, we've got to be right on top of whatever it is. We're not even all digging, there's only three shovels for six of us, everyone pitched in their fair share, now could a couple of us borrow your car and get to town? You can see the smoke, we're not making it up to get out of helping you."

Their overseer ignored the question, his doughy cheeks sagging. "All's I'm saying is a deal is a deal. If we're right on top of it, it should only take a minute more. Plus there's a chance this isn't even the right spot."

"Sounds like something an assassin would say right before offing us all," said Benny, sitting with his arms crossed across his legs while he watched Mark, Tom, and Kaela digging. The man swung his head around to glare at Benny, apparently offended, but then smiled. Benny focused his attention on Tom and, out of sheer awkwardness, asked "Did you ever open up your time capsule, Tom?"

Tom looked up at him and furrowed his brow, putting his weight on the shovel.

"Oh yeah, hey, it's a good thing you found it before the island burned down," said Ann.

"Tell us what was inside," said Mark as he wiped sweat from his brow.

Tad hooked a mud-covered sneaker on a mound of dirt and looked at Tom with patient attention, showing interest in the mysterious contents as well.

Tom sighed in irritation. "There wasn't a time capsule at all. I just wanted time away from you guys."

"Jesus Christ, Tom. Believe me, nobody regrets coming up here more than me," said Kaela.

"Cat would have hated it up here," said Tom, almost too quietly to hear but not quite.

"Fuck off Tom," said Mark. "Cat would have liked it."

Kaela paused digging and looked over at Tom, her eyes distant as though channeling what Cat's opinion would have been. Tad was also watching Tom, trying to catch his eye, but when Tom looked back his eyes were dark, tired, and emotionless; sharklike, his thoughts too hard to parse from the outside in. "If we dig a couple more feet, that will be enough to know if it's here for sure, and then you'll get your ride," said Tad.

"What if this is the wrong spot?" asked Mark.

Tad checked their position, calibrating a certain distance between the cabin and a blue wooden toadstool near the edge of the woods. "It shouldn't be an issue. But work faster, if the ground freezes it will be that much harder to dig. When we get to town the coffee is on me," he added in an afterthought.

The ground was not yet frozen, but the soil was still dense, tightly packed, possibly never before disturbed. Their bodies ached, none of them prepared and all of them too hungover for such a task, starving for more Bloody Mary's. But they pushed through, with a growing curiosity over what they were digging up. A hope that Brooke and Moody might be back at any time with help in tow began to settle across the group as well. Growing excited, Tad asked for Kaela's shovel and began working at a frenzied pace, as though he had been reserving his energy for that very moment, the home stretch. The condensation on his clothes had become frosted by the freezing temperature and crunched with his first movements, the ice cracking and falling off him in small bits.

The other two eased off from shoveling, their shovel heads getting in the way of Tad's intense digging. The group circled around him, now genuinely interested to see what was there. Tad's small eyes began to dart across them with increasing frequency and his manner became jumpy; at one point the shovel struck something solid, sounding a loud clang and he jumped a foot. "There's nothing here yet," he said, laughing but grimacing as he threw the large rock to the side. His feverish dig continued for several more minutes before he showed signs of slowing.

"All right man," said Mark. "I hate to say it but it looks like this spot is a no go? It has to be at least five feet deep, how far down could this thing be?"

"No, we're so close! We can't stop now," laughed Tad.

"But no one else is even digging. We're all just watching you and seriously, we have important shit to do," said Tom.

Tad looked at them in surprise, then quickly crumbled into rage. "We're not going anywhere until I find what I need."

"That's fucking it," said Benny. "Let's just hold this guy down and take his keys."

They advanced on Tad, who had no escape from the slim chamber he had dug himself into, but then recoiled before reaching down to him, remembering the bulk inside his pocket. In that moment of hesitation Tad collapsed into a ball to stop them from lifting him out, but they dragged him out regardless of his solid dead weight.

"You're never going to find the car key on me, I hid it," screeched Tad as he kicked and swung at them, finally answering the question of whether he had a gun. Mark, Tom, and Benny pinned him down by the arms and legs while Kaela and Ann frisked him for the keys or any weapons, but they found neither.

"There's nothing here, he's telling the truth," groaned Kaela.

"Go look for his car, the key is probably under a tire of somewhere close by, we'll keep him here," said Tom.

Kaela and Ann ran down the driveway, their feet crunching through the already inch deep accumulation of snow. They had been kept warm from digging but the cold was beginning to sink into their bones. "Where did he say he parked it?" asked Ann when they reached the road.

They looked in each direction but didn't see a car. "He said he was parked past the driveway, but he didn't say which way. Let's split up, just give a shout if you spot it first." They took off jogging in opposite directions, casting glances into the woods on both sides as they searched. Kaela reached a curve in the road and looked back to check how far Ann had gone but she was out of sight, Ann having already rounded her own curve. After a couple of minutes, she began to feel a stitch in her side and switched pace to a fast walk, regretting not taking up running as a hobby. She realized that the distance to the car's hiding spot depended on how paranoid Tad was, which seemed to be quite high, and that she and Ann should have agreed on how far to search ahead of time. After ten minutes she gave up and began heading back, hoping that Ann had found the car in her direction.

The return trip was peaceful, almost otherworldly. The leaves were still falling from the trees, intermingling with the snowfall drifting down from the grey sky. Green grass poked up through the ground, which was scattered with a gradient of autumnal shades. Brown, red, orange, yellow, white, and green. Having such a sour experience on something meant to honor Cat had been too much; she was unlikely to invite other people to the cabin again, if she ever even went back herself. As she considered whether this would be her final trip, she paused for a moment to savor the view and stood in the middle of the dirt road, letting the snow collect on her clothes and hair.

There was no sign of Ann when she reached the driveway and she did the last bit of the trek up the driveway on her own, thinking maybe Ann had not waited for her and could already be back with the keys. As she approached she could see Mark, Tom, and Benny shoveling dirt back into the hole.

"I couldn't find the car, I walked until it seemed like too far – Ann and I split up to search in both directions – did she come back yet? Did she find the key?"

"No, she hasn't come back yet, we should probably start walking whichever way she went, and then we should really just keep going that way to figure out where Moody and Brooke wound up," said Mark as they began to walk towards the driveway.

"Wait, where is the guy?" she asked, looking around hyper-vigilantly.

"He took off," said Benny. "He managed to get out of our grip, cussed us out and went running back into the woods."

"What a freakshow," said Kaela. "Hold on, I want to grab a water from inside."

"I've got one here for you," said Mark.

They waited for her to take a drink, adjusting their coats and backpacks in the meantime. She screwed the cap back on. "Everybody out here has a pick-up truck, someone will be able to pull the van out even if there isn't a towing company. Good thing we held off on loading it up or it might be too heavy."

"Well, actually we went ahead and loaded it up. But nothing was that heavy, it should be fine," said Mark.

"And no need to look around for every little thing," said Tom. "I'm thinking of moving up here, for a little while anyway. This place will fall apart without someone here to take care of it."

"What?! That would be crazy, Tom. Plus, I kind of need your half of the rent for the apartment."

"It's okay, I'll come down, get my stuff, and come back up with my car. I'll give you my share of the rent for the rest of the lease. I have enough saved up."

Kaela stopped to picture Tom alone in the cabin over the winter but was too exhausted to argue and nodded, deciding to pursue the topic on the drive home.

As they walked closer to the road they saw Ann approaching. She jogged up to close the distance and asked, "Did you find the car your way?"

"No, and please tell me you're joking," answered Kaela.

"I'm not. *Fuck.* If he didn't have a car, how did he even get here?"

"Maybe he actually lives somewhere close by. He could be your new neighbor if you move up here, Tom," said Mark cheerfully. "Maybe I'll give him some money to sucker punch you as payback for earlier. By the way, he got away."

"Seriously? You mean he could be out there watching us right now?" Ann asked, her eyes flitting from tree to tree. "Let's get out of here, let's just start walking to town. This way, this is the direction those two would be coming back from."

"We'd better keep moving, it gets the blood pumping and will keep us warm," said Benny, walking briskly ahead.

Tom looked around at the dusting of snow on the dirt road and suddenly asked, "Have you guys noticed that it seems like the sun is brighter than it was when we were kids? I swear, it's lighter than it used to be. Even in the daytime."

Benny handed Ann her backpack and a water as they started walking away, each of them searching for signs of their friends or Tad throughout the hours-long walk they had to reach the store. By that time the island was surely in cinders, with everything living and non-living obliterated. But the fire was contained by the lake, relieving them of urgency to find help; the damage was already done. The coil of smoke in the sky grew darker and denser even as they walked further away. They could hear the occasional car pass on the other side of the woods, the mechanical whir a comfort as it sounded through the forest.

During the walk they began joking about the horrible weekend until they were near tears with laughter over how horrendous it was. Kaela was delighted, the creation of a new chapter of group lore made the trip worthwhile, the experience given value through the sheer number of things gone wrong. Thrilled and convinced that Cat herself would have been pleased, she kept laughing to herself sporadically even after the others had stopped, as her mind darted back to the man in the woods and the guys refilling the hole.

Acknowledgements

A special thank you to the following creators whose work I borrowed most heavily from: Algernon Blackwood and Morgalla Dodai Stewart.

Additional thanks go out to my family for supporting me (especially my husband) as I wrote this and to all of the teachers that have helped me along the way.

And thank you, reader, for being there.